# "Ryan Is Your Son, Bryce. I've Brought Him Back To You."

Bryce seemed to explode at Marlie from across the room, one moment a rock of impenetrable stillness, the next, a rush of intensely heated ire. His hands gripped her arms until her bones ached. His face pressed near hers, a mask of ugly accusations and disbelief. "You're lying."

Fear writhed in the pit of her stomach. Yet, with vivid clarity, she understood and sympathized with his contradicting emotions. Bryce was afraid to believe. She touched his face with gentle fingertips, instilling a sense of reality to her words. "He's alive, Bryce. Ryan is your son."

Dear Reader,

Welcome to March! Spring is in the air. The birds are chirping, the bees are buzzing... and men and women all over the world are thinking about—love.

Here at Silhouette Desire we take love *very* seriously. We're committed to bringing you six terrific stories all about love each and every month of the year, and this March is no exception.

Let's start with March's *Man of the Month* by Jackie Merritt. It's called *Tennessee Waltz*, and I know you're going to love this story. Next, Naomi Horton returns with *Chastity's Pirate*. (How can you resist a book with a title like this? You just *can't!*) And look for books by Anne Marie Winston, Barbara McCauley, Justine Davis and new-to-Desire Kat Adams.

And in months to come, some of your very favorite authors are coming your way. Look for sensuous romances from the talented pens of Dixie Browning, Lass Small, Cait London, Barbara Boswell... just to name a few.

So go wild with Desire, and start thinking about love.

All the best,

Lucia Macro
Senior Editor

# KAT ADAMS

# THURSDAY'S CHILD

SILHOUETTE *Desire*

Published by Silhouette Books New York

America's Publisher of Contemporary Romance

**SILHOUETTE BOOKS**
300 East 42nd St., New York, N.Y. 10017

THURSDAY'S CHILD

Copyright © 1993 by Kat Adams

All rights reserved. Except for use in any review, the reproduction or utilization of this work in whole or in part in any form by any electronic, mechanical or other means, now known or hereafter invented, including xerography, photocopying and recording, or in any information storage or retrieval system, is forbidden without the permission of the publisher, Silhouette Books, 300 E. 42nd St., New York, N.Y. 10017

ISBN: 0-373-05773-3

First Silhouette Books printing March 1993

All the characters in this book have no existence outside the imagination of the author and have no relation whatsoever to anyone bearing the same name or names. They are not even distantly inspired by any individual known or unknown to the author, and all incidents are pure invention.

® and ™: Trademarks used with authorization. Trademarks indicated with ® are registered in the United States Patent and Trademark Office, the Canada Trade Mark Office and in other countries.

Printed in the U.S.A.

**Books by Kat Adams**

Silhouette Romance

*Love Bug* #463
*The Ace of Hearts* #788
*The Price of Paradise* #810

Silhouette Desire

*Thursday's Child* #773

---

# KAT ADAMS

was always an enthusiastic reader of romances. To her, coming home to a good romance was like leaving the Twilight Zone of housekeeping and entering Disneyland. Eventually, she decided that if reading romances was pleasurable, then writing them would be pure delight.

# Prologue

---

Marlena Stynhearst had never thought she'd be comparing herself to something as disgusting as a cornered rat, but that was exactly how she was feeling. She was literally backed against the wall of her own fortress. As her eyes swept the posh furnishings of her Los Angeles office, she found her little kingdom lacked anything that might help her now. Words were her only defense, words and a grit that had sprung up from the terrible sensation of being duped.

"You're insane, Rex," she snapped, fighting to release her hands from his shackling fist.

"You'd like to believe that, wouldn't you, Marlena?" he murmured against the soft flesh beneath her ear. "But it's just greed. You're a product of greed, darling. You understand."

Marlena shivered. A month ago this man's touch would have sent a welcomed, tantalizing chill over her body. Tonight, the chill was there, but it was one of revulsion. With a bravado that sounded ridiculous given her present position, she replied frostily, "No, I don't understand. My brother was supposed to have been your friend, yet I learn that you had coerced him out of enormous control of Stynhearst Industries. Is that what you've planned for me? I'll warn you, you'll not find *me* so easily managed."

Rex Kane chuckled, ignoring her starchy declaration. "Andrew was a fool. He allowed his obsession with gambling and his demanding wife to manipulate him." His amusement swept into a laugh of demonic gusto. "You know, I wish old Andrew were still around so I could send him a thank-you note. It was truly considerate of him to get himself and his nuisance of a wife killed in that accident three years ago. The company people had begun to wonder why he didn't show more interest in the business. Now, with Andrew and Eva dead and Stynhearst in your hands, no one thinks it strange that the pretty young heiress has fallen madly in love with her CEO."

Marlena found a sneer came easily when turned on the despised deeds of an enemy. "I did fall into your hands like a ripe plum, didn't I?" she demanded bitterly.

"Oh, darling, don't be so hard on yourself," he crooned in feigned commiseration. "After Andrew's death, you were so wrapped up in taking care of your orphaned nephew and finishing your last two years of college that you allowed me to take over even more control of Stynhearst. You did the logical thing. The thing I was counting on you to do."

"And wasn't it so generous of you to offer to personally show me the ropes of Stynhearst after I graduated, all the while pretending to fall in love with me?" Marlena added, aggrieved by her own gullibility.

"It's my irresistible charm, darling," Rex murmured. He used his free hand to whisk aside her long brunette curls so he could roam the territory of her exposed throat. "Remember to be more careful the next time a man uses it on you."

"You can be certain I will." She turned away from his descending mouth, not attempting to hide her repugnance to his touch. "I promise I'll not soon forget any of your lessons, Rex," she whispered.

He drew back, tightening the hold on her wrists until she thought they would snap. "You're not a fool, Marlena, so remember this lesson," he growled, laying his free hand upon her breast. "If you don't give me everything my little heart desires, I'll see to it that you lose your little heart's desire."

Ryan. He was speaking of her nephew, Ryan. Marlena's heart beat in frantic dread, but still she couldn't back down. "Your smugness is premature, Rex. Don't forget I found the tape of you telling Andrew that the child he thought he'd adopted had actually been stolen from a couple in Connecticut." She looked at her former friend and fiancé, unable to believe the depths of his duplicity. "Every time you wanted something, you used that tape to threaten Andrew with losing Ryan."

Rex rolled his eyes upward and sighed in dramatic bliss. "Isn't love marvelous, darling? When used properly, it can lay the world at one's feet. All it takes is a victim who's willing to sacrifice everything in the name of love. In this case, it was our own dear Andy who sacrificed Stynhearst for the love of his gambling, his wife's money to pay his debts and his best friend—me—who provided the child, which kept Eva happy."

He ran his knuckles along the ridge of her cheek. "If you'd not been so nosy, darling, you'd never have known you were sacrificing Stynhearst for Ryan. But you had to snoop around in my safe. Looking for the boy's birth certificate?" he guessed.

When she nodded hesitantly, he continued. "I'd gotten Ryan into that fancy school for gifted children last year without one, didn't I? What made you think I couldn't do so again?"

Marlena jerked away from his hand. It amazed her how he could flit through trifling details while disregarding the magnitude of his atrocious actions. "What kind of monster are you?" she hissed. "You kidnapped a baby to use in trapping my brother, then you secretly taped that conversation between yourself and Andrew where you confessed to taking Ryan. With the tape, you had proof that Andrew was aware of Ryan's true parentage, and by Andrew's silence, he as good as sanctioned your crime."

"Very good, Marlena. I knew you were a smart girl. So, you must also understand that now that you've listened to the tape and know the truth about Ryan, you've replaced Andrew in that same incriminating boat."

Green eyes as hard and glittery as emeralds bore into Rex Kane with little effect. Yes, I have replaced my brother in that boat, haven't I? she impotently seethed in silence. After listening to the tape, she'd had no doubts as to why Rex had held on to the damning evidence. Tonight her theory had proven correct. Rex was using it to give her an ultimatum: marry him, allow him complete control of Stynhearst, or lose Ryan.

She hiked her chin up a notch. "Your blackmail is double-edged, though, Rex. You can't take Ryan away from me, because if you do, I'll use the tape to implicate you in his kidnapping."

He shrugged. "Andrew tried that approach with me. I'll tell you what I told him. I've spent the last four years using that little boy to gain control of Stynhearst. You can turn the tape over to the police, and I'll end up losing everything and spending time in jail." He used his tall, muscular body to crowd her closer into the corner, then whispered, "But the authorities would be duty-bound to return little Ryan to his grief-stricken parents, wouldn't they, darling? Can you give up Ryan?"

A futile hate left Marlena standing in muted helplessness.

"I don't think you can, Marlena," he continued speculatively. "You're so transparent, so easily read. I knew by that strange mood swing you experienced a week ago that something was wrong. When I discovered the tape and newspaper article of the kidnapping missing from my safe, I had my answer. For a week I watched you struggle with indecision. For a whole week you've known the truth, but—" he tipped up her chin until she was forced to meet his eyes "—you haven't told anyone, have you? If you haven't found the nerve to turn the evidence over to the police yet, then I don't think you will."

No, she hadn't found the nerve. Ryan's natural parents had known him eighteen months before they'd lost him. Andrew and Eva had claimed an equal amount of time in Ryan's life. But Marlena had held that child in her arms for three wonderful years. Though no biological ties existed between them, she and Ryan shared a kinship that ran deeper than the bonds of blood. Marlena had at last found a family in Ryan, and to Ryan, she was his rock in a world of shifting sand. They needed each other; it was as simple as that.

Now her life was being swept up in a fiendish eddy of fear created by one man's evilness. She was being forced to fight a battle against him that she could not win, but would not surrender. "I won't marry you, Rex," she responded defiantly. "Even if I don't turn you in, I'll still not marry you and give you this company."

An unnerving smile settled on Rex's lips. His fingers found the pulse points of her throat and applied enough pressure to communicate a warning. "I admire your bravery, but you are so very naive. You see, darling, like Andrew, I enjoy gambling, but I play for even higher stakes. In this game I'm playing with you, I'm betting on an all-or-nothing proposition. I'll either forfeit my position and my freedom, or I'll gain the whole company and its beautiful heiress as my bride."

He chuckled as he turned his threatening grasp into a parody of a caress. "I can see by the look on your face that you're beginning to understand me. That's good. A wife should understand her husband."

He abruptly shifted his arm, snaring Marlena's waist. He made sure that this time, his kiss wouldn't be denied. He ground his lips against hers, hurting her, subduing her with his superior strength. She struggled, but he followed her movement with painful persistence, allowing her no relief from the suffocating pressure of his body.

Just when Marlena thought she'd faint from the lack of breath, he loosened his hold but kept her within the circle of his arm. He taunted her with his supremacy. "Tomorrow, you will return the tape and the news article to me. In a few weeks, we'll marry as planned. After our honeymoon, you will begin the process of turning over full reign of Stynhearst Industries to me. Then you can continue being a little mother to the boy. You will be managed, Marlena, *or you will lose Ryan.*"

His finger traced the length of the gold chain around her neck, following its links to where they disappeared between her breasts as he leisurely added, "I might point out that there are several ways to lose a child. I never got around to producing any legal documents, such as Ryan's adoption papers and birth certificate. Without them, Andrew couldn't even claim the boy as his son. So, as far as the world is concerned, Ryan ceased to exist several years ago. I can easily make that a fact, Marlena."

His hand moved behind his back, then suddenly reappeared, holding a knife before her eyes. Marlena stiffened as the shiny blade winked at her with macabre seductiveness before vanishing from her sight. "Just so you won't misjudge the limits of my ambition, darling."

The knife pressed against the side of Marlena's hip, hissing as it severed the fabric of her skirt and almost delicately nipped into the flesh beneath. A small whimper escaped her throat, more from fright than pain, as the wound awakened her to the reality of how far this man would go to force her into submission.

"I'll enjoy admiring that little scar on our honeymoon, Marlena," he purred, then released her and started for the door. "I'm glad I decided to initiate this little discussion tonight. You'd stewed long enough, and I wanted to relieve your mind by letting you know that everything is settled."

He swung around once more to face her. "Oh. One more lesson before I leave, darling," he said. "You allowed yourself to become too attached to Ryan and it cost you. Never care for someone to the point that they become indispensable."

The door closed, leaving Marlena in the stark loneliness of dealing with her plight. She touched her hip, then examined the blood on her fingertips dispassionately. Rex Kane had made two mistakes this evening. One, he naturally assumed that all people's selfishness and greed, whatever form they took, rivaled his own. And two, he had threatened Ryan's life.

The combination of these two errors would cause Rex Kane's downfall—Marlena would see to it. For although Rex was right, she did love Ryan desperately and did find him indispensable to her existence, she would not allow Rex to use Ryan as a pawn.

To protect Ryan, Marlena would have to give him up.

She had known for days that this was inevitable. Ryan's parents deserved their child back after four and a half anguish-filled years. Rex Kane deserved to forfeit ten times as many years of his freedom in payment for that anguish.

She picked up the phone, intending to seek the advice of her attorney, but dropped it back into its cradle before she completed the call. Rex's words rang like a death knell inside her head: the moment the authorities learn Ryan's identity, they would whisk him away to his parents.

Marlie ran her fingers through her tangled hair in agitation. She needed time. Time to make certain Ryan was going to a good home. Time to meet Ryan's parents, to get to know them and they to know her, before she reintroduced them to their son.

Then, if she had properly paved the way for understanding, maybe Bryce and Janette Powell would find room in Ryan's new life for an illegitimate Aunt Marlie.

# One

*Honk! Honk! Honk!*

Marlena Theodora Stynhearst—or just plain Marlie now, since her recent topple from society—gave the irate motorist behind her an equally irate scowl via the sideview mirror of her stalled pickup truck. Having done her dirtiest retaliation for the moment, she continued fanning herself with a Connecticut road map and contemplating why it was in such bad taste to feel sorry for oneself. Personally, she thought she'd more than earned the right.

*Slap . . . slap . . . slap.*

"That guy behind us is extremely rude, isn't he, Aunt Marlie?"

Marlie smiled feebly across the worn truck seat at her young nephew who was contenting himself with slapping a baseball into his mitted hand. She knew better than to totally concur with Ryan Bartholomew Stynhearst's assessment of the honker's manners. Ryan could appear as angelic as one of Gabriel's own, with a little ball cap squashing his adorable curls into a golden halo around his head. Marlie knew better, though. This intellectually brilliant six-year-old knew such diabolical means of seeking restitution that it made her skin crawl. She tempered her agreement with an attempt at charity that she hoped the honker behind her appreciated.

"It's terribly hot, Ryan," she explained patiently. "Heat has a way of bringing out the beast in all of us." She could tell this recital of adult logic had no appreciable effect on the child. Ryan, as with most children, had a natural immunity to environmental conditions that drove grown-ups crazy. She tried another approach. "He's probably in a hurry to get home to his wonderful swimming pool and a cold can of root beer."

Ryan pursed his lips, squinted his big blue eyes and furrowed his brow, a prelude to the dreaded *w* word. "Why doesn't he just back up and go another way, then?" he demanded, clearly put out with anyone who couldn't figure out a simple solution to the problem.

Marlie was left with her usual, inadequate response. "I don't know."

She also didn't know why she had to come up with the bright idea of talking that sweet old man, who was selling produce on the corner across from the Sunnydale bus station, into letting her rent his truck for a few hours, either. She could have carried the six suitcases of paraphernalia she and Ryan had accumulated on their trip easier than fighting this mean-natured truck.

Five minutes had passed since the truck conked out in the middle of the alley, leaving them sweltering in the early-July heat. A helpful young man at a gas station had suggested this alley as a shortcut to the only motel across town. Of course, he'd neglected to mention the potholes as big as moon craters dotting the alley. The last pothole she'd hit must have shaken loose something important in the truck, for it had figuratively put its foot down and refused to budge.

*Slap...slap...slap.*
*Honk! Honk! Honk!*

Marlie squeezed her eyes shut and continued fanning herself with one hand while massaging her throbbing temple with the other. What am I doing here? she silently moaned. But she knew all too well what she was doing here.

From California to Connecticut, Marlie's trail had been one of silent tears and constant reminders of what lay at the end—she was going to lose Ryan. This knowledge worried her consciousness like a diagnosed cancer. And anticipating its consequences to her life evoked a fear that closely resembled hopelessness. She was going to lose Ryan, and the best of herself would be lost with him.

She watched Ryan fidget with childish energy and marveled at how she could have been so blessed with his appearance in her life. Ryan needed her, and through him, she vicariously relived the first fourteen years of her contented childhood with Nanny Jane.

Marlie smiled, thinking of darling Jane Pritchett. Jane had been another one of those blessings that Marlie didn't take for granted. The kindly old lady had raised Marlie from infancy when her parents had refused to be fettered by their inconvenient offspring. Thanks to Nanny Jane, Marlie had lived a delightful childhood, full of fun and excitement and learning. Nanny Jane used every opportunity possible to throw open the doors of Marlie's dreary mansion, introducing her charge to fascinating people and experiences.

And along the way Nanny Jane shared her wisdom, teaching Marlie the joys of generosity, the character of compassion and the fulfillment of love. For fourteen years, she was Marlie's family, the two existing in an ordinary world that insulated the child against the more cruel elements of life.

The day Marlie had stood beside her parents flower-decked caskets, she had said a final farewell to those two strangers. And then she said a final farewell to her beloved Nanny Jane.

Andrew, a brother ten years Marlie's senior, couldn't be bothered with a sister he scarcely knew. Nanny Jane was getting old and past her usefulness, Andrew had said. Much better that a budding adolescent of society's elite be tutored in the finer schools of Europe. Without remorse he dismissed the old nanny and sentenced Marlie to four lonely, fearful, disillusioning years at a small, exclusive boarding school in France.

Marlie knew there were many nice, rich people; her new schoolmates were not. Tossed among children whose values and principles were not her own, Marlie soon learned that she must swim with conformity or sink into isolation.

Mostly, Marlie sank.

She couldn't get the hang of judging people according to their position on the social register. She couldn't find the expected satisfaction from vicious gossip or petty revenge. She tried feasting on her worldly possessions and found herself starving for spiritual substance. To her female peers, Marlie was strange—a square peg trying to fit into a round hole. Of course her male peers didn't care if she was strange; she was attractive and rich . . . and fair game.

In the classroom, Marlie drew upon the strength instilled by Nanny Jane and showed the world a smiling face that hid her inner fears. In the dormitory, she learned to live behind a closed door, with loneliness as her closest companion. But always present were the toughness and pride that sustained her ideals and convictions. Marlie survived those four years, but she would never forget them.

Boarding school ended and still she couldn't go home. Go home to what? A brother she didn't know and who didn't want to know her? To a life-style that didn't fit? So she entered a small British university, and studying became her passionate escape from the loneliness of rejection.

The news of Andrew and his wife's accident saddened Marlie, yet with their deaths new life blossomed in her heart. She went home. Home to the wonderful discovery that she was an aunt. Three-year-old Ryan scampered into her life, wearing Spiderman training pants and a dimpled smile that put the silver lining back into Marlie's clouds.

Ryan chased away her bitter, frightening memories of being different from the crowd. Gone were the feelings of uselessness and rejection, the loneliness and fear of being uprooted like a hothouse flower and transplanted on cold, foreign soil. Ryan loved her and needed her, and Marlie soon got back into the business of living life with a purpose again. Recreating the familiar environment of her childhood, Marlie passed on to Ryan Nanny Jane's beautiful legacy of love and devotion, and together aunt and nephew flourished.

Now the hopes of the future were blighted by uncertainties. Marlie twisted the road map in her damp hands, wondering about the Powells. Could they be tolerant, forgiving or accommodating enough to share what Marlie needed most? She needed the child who loved her without reservation, who needed her and allowed her to love him—the child who kept the ghost of her fear of aloneness at bay.

These things she needed, but not more than the greater need to protect the provider. Therefore, she was going to lose Ryan.

The stifling heat of the unair-conditioned truck had kissed the child's freckled nose with beads of sweat. Marlie drank in the sight of the brace of dimples that dented his cheeks as he concentrated on the precision timing of the ball hitting his mitt. Emotion swelled in her throat until she thought it would strangle her. Dear Lord, she loved this child. What would she do when he was gone? *You can't do this,* her brittle bravery fretted. But she would.

"What's wrong, Aunt Marlie?" the boy asked with concern. "Is that guy behind us getting on your nerves?" *Slap... slap... slap.*

Admonishing herself to snap out of this useless melancholy, she reverted to a more typical behavior. "Ryan," she said in controlled exasperation. "You only know the half of it. I can't start this stupid truck. I can't stop the honker behind me. But I can stop the monotonous racket inside this cab." She plucked the mitt from his hand and slapped it on the seat between them.

The slapping stopped. The honking didn't.

"Want me to have a look under the hood?" Ryan asked, now amusing himself with repeatedly pitching the ball into the air. "It's probably either Carl Carburetor or Bobby Battery."

Marlie stared at him blankly. He informed her, "I know engine parts don't really have proper names, but it helps to remember them."

Right, she thought wryly.

*Honk! Honk! Honk!*

"I'm going to have to find a mechanic," she muttered wearily.

"What are you going to do about the rude guy behind us?" Ryan asked, thumbing in that direction.

"Do you happen to have a hand grenade in there?" she asked, nudging his duffel bag, which she assumed was filled with boy-type essentials.

Ryan gave her a perplexed look, for though he was a bright lad, it was his aunt who held the honors in subtle sarcasm. "Never mind," she said, grinning and waving away her inquiry. "I'll just have to take the wind out of our honker's sails another way."

Ryan's blue eyes lit up with interest. "Can I help?"

Not knowing how friendly the confrontation between the ill-tempered honker and the damsel in distress would be, Marlie shook her head. "I can handle him alone. Thanks."

Ryan looked disappointed. Marlie smiled as she released the door latch and leapt lightly to the rough surface of the alley. She took a moment to smooth back loose brunette strands into her drooping ponytail while reconnoitering the alley. Marlie had viewed three thousand miles of American scenery after it had already passed her by, for she had spent the four-week trip looking over her shoulder. Rex Kane was out there. Sooner or later he would find her, and she would prefer to meet him face-to-face, rather than have him sneak up from behind.

But Rex Kane wasn't her problem in this alley; the person cursing her in car-horn language was. She set a militant pace to the maroon Saab parked almost on the bumper of her truck.

*Honk! Honk—*

The last honk of the standard three was cut off as if Marlie's sudden appearance had robbed it of its audacity. Using a neatly manicured fingernail, she tapped on the tinted glass separating her from the driver. The window immediately descended with a soft burr of motion. She pasted on a conservative smile and stooped to look her tormentor in the eye. In this case it turned out to be aviator sunglasses, so she focused intently on her own reflection in them and said sweetly, "Since this arrangement is getting us nowhere, I have a suggestion. Why don't you start my truck for me, and I'll blow your horn for you?"

The sunglasses tilted as the male wearing them considered her from a new angle. A tentative smile appeared, then grew a tad bolder, poking dimples into his bristly cheeks. Always a sucker for a pair of dimples, Marlie took a closer look at her honker. What she saw tempted a grin of her own. Honker was good-looking. Very good-looking in a sweaty ball cap, five o'clock shadow sort of way.

*Back off, Stynhearst,* she warned herself. A woman with the instincts of a kamikaze pilot when it came to judging the opposite sex had no business giving a male the once-over.

Still, Marlie couldn't help but be intrigued by the man. His smile was wary, with a dash of vulnerability that knocked on the door of her heart. She could relate to wariness and vulnerability. But with enough troubles on her mind she turned a deaf ear to the echoes in her heart and firmly suppressed the urge to return his smile. Instead she raised an eyebrow, challenging him to either admit he was a cad or do something about it.

"I made a mistake," he said by way of meager apology.

Marlie nodded. "Yes, you have, if you think blowing your car horn will intimidate my truck into starting." She turned on the voltage of a deceptively charming smile. "You can see for yourself that it doesn't work."

The lips of the handsome honker twitched again. "That wasn't the mistake I made," he said evenly. "My mistake was thinking you were another one of those annoying people who have the idea that this alley is a parking lot. I've had to turn around three times this week. But today I was hot, tired and feeling just mean enough not to take the long way home."

He paused, gauging her degree of sympathy. Marlie raised a hand to delicately pat away a bored yawn, though her green eyes twinkled with laconic humor at the cad's expense.

He launched a counterattack by pulling off his sunglasses and turned on her two blue eyes that could talk a woman into anything." We also just lost our ball game by one lousy run," he added morosely.

If Marlie had still been a pushover, she may have bought that line and taken the owner of the blue eyes as a bonus. Thanks to her recent education in men, their lines and their looks, she more prudently evaluated what was being offered. She decided she didn't think much of it. "Life can sure be the devil sometimes, can't it?" she responded, pitilessly laughing at his sad tale.

"It's refreshing to find a female who appreciates the delicacy of the male ego," he said dryly. "I have a few tools in my trunk. How about if I give my horn a rest while I take a look at your truck?"

Before she could agree or disagree, he swung open his door, forcing her to step back. Her false smile fell from her face, and she retreated another step as the man straightened to his full height. Rex Kane was six feet tall, but this man would top him by three easy inches. Rex Kane was well built, but this man had more muscles than he could possibly know what to do with. She touched the scar on the side of her hip, vividly recalling the advantages of a man's superior strength. For one heartbeat of time, she intensely resented this man for inspiring the recollection of her helplessness.

Then, just as quickly, the debilitating sensation passed. Slinking off like a simp every time she met someone taller than herself would be admitting that Rex still controlled her life. She absolutely refused to allow it. Nothing was going to mar her remaining time with Ryan. To prove her mettle she turned her attention back to this unnecessarily large male who was standing in the same pothole with her.

His long legs were encased in a pair of those stretchy stirrup pants that ball players wear, his tapered torso plastered with a green jersey. A fashionable length of glossy dark hair fringed a green ball cap, and from the amount of dirt and sweat accentuating all that evident virility, Marlie surmised that he wasn't kidding about the ball game. "You do play ball," she stated unnecessarily, wanting to hear again the pleasant resonance of his Yankee accent.

"Yep," he said over his shoulder as he walked to the rear of his car, unlocked the trunk and retrieved the tools. "And I really am a sore loser, too."

As he passed her on his way to her truck, she tried to check her recoiling steps, but couldn't. She consoled herself by suggesting that there was nothing cowardly about keeping a sensible distance from anything that big and obviously badtempered. Like a little caboose, she trailed behind the man, inquiring politely, "So you were taking your defeat and resulting nastiness out on me and my poor little truck?"

"That's about the size of it," he said with a gruff economy of words.

They reached the truck before Marlie had time to stick out her tongue at the boorish man's back. He handed her the tools, propped his sunglasses on the bill of his cap, then swung open the heavy truck hood with little effort. The damp ball uniform clung to the contours of his muscular body, providing the means for an exhibition in kinetic poetry, while proving his ability to use the power at his disposal. Marlie watched him, experiencing the fear and fascination of a foolish mortal tempted to stroke the beautiful, wild beast.

She swallowed heavily, told herself not to be silly and climbed upon the bumper opposite of where he tinkered with the mystical conglomeration of metal gadgetry. Focusing intently on his busy hands, she asked absently, "Do you think it's Carl Carburetor or Bobby Battery causing the problem?"

The man slowly raised his head to stare at her, and she was subjected to another whammy from those piercing blue eyes. Then his chest began to heave, building pressure for an awesome explosion. It happened, in fact. Reluctant laughter came barreling out, robbing the man of his strength until he had to grasp the truck frame to retain his balance.

Marlie crossed her arms over her chest and patiently waited until the storm of his hilarity calmed. She raised a convincingly disdainful eyebrow. "I know engine parts don't really have proper names, but it helps to remember them." She haughtily quoted Ryan's wisdom.

His smile came easier and more sincerely, as if now that he had finally tried one on for size he found it comfortable. How strange, she thought. She had forty-two sweet little inches worth of reason to smile waiting for her in the truck; even Rex Kane's despicable greed couldn't take that from her. What reason could this obviously healthy, obviously wealthy man have for being so stingy with his humor?

"Sorry if I hurt your feelings," he said, his lips still twitching. "It was just the idea of a little commune residing under the hood of a vehicle that set me off." He leaned over the engine again and added whimsically, "I'd say Connie Coil Wire is our culprit here. You must have disconnected her from Dennis Distributor when you hit the last pothole."

The dimples disappeared again and Marlie thought that rather a shame. To coax them back she tried, "Sounds as if Connie and Dennis were engaged in immoral behavior, anyway. What happens when they disconnect?"

It worked; he repeated that brilliant white smile and augmented it with a wink. "Nothing. Unless Connie is attached...intimately to Dennis, the sparks won't fly. No sparks, no action."

The hesitant smiler had just graduated to a prospective flirt. Marlie decided to quit while she was ahead. She forced her eyes to break their own intimate connection with his. "I believe a union of such significance calls for the assistance of a professional. If you can point me in the direction of a good mechanic, I'll thank you and let you be on your way."

"No need for that." He reached into the truck innards, fiddled a few moments with—Connie and Dennis?—then straightened with a satisfied grunt. "Reunited at last," he said. "You'll start now."

Marlie was impressed. "Thank you," she said, grinning.

She stepped off the bumper and wiped the dust from her hands onto the seat of her cutoff jeans. She had expected the man to rush off to wherever, but he leaned a hand on the truck, crossing his ankles in a relaxed stance that bespoke of nothing but time on his hands. "I couldn't help noticing that this old truck looks exactly like Happy Hanson's," he commented leisurely.

Marlie nodded. "Happy Hanson being the man who sells produce on one of the decently paved streets in this town and who rented me this ornery contraption to move my luggage from the bus station to the motel."

His grimness was back. "You're just passing through Sunnydale?"

She shrugged. "Not exactly. I'll be staying for a few weeks, but the motel will be my address until I find an apartment."

His blue eyes took a visual tour down the length of Marlie's body en route to the toes of his cleated shoes, which he regarded for several moments. Finally he looked at her and remarked, "There's only one apartment complex in Sunnydale."

Marlie was starting to get the message of why he was hanging around and refused to encourage him. "There seems to be only one of everything in Sunnydale," she replied flatly.

"There's only one vacant town house in that one apartment complex," he persisted.

"I'd better hurry then," she countered meaningfully.

Now that he'd gotten the hang of smiling, he didn't seem to want to turn it off. "You're within about twenty potholes of your destination. The rear of the apartments run parallel with this alley. I'll follow you over and tell Mrs. Cobb that I recommend you as a tenant."

"You don't even know me," Marlie protested, surprised.

"I like what I've seen so far." To prove it, he took another thorough look.

With renditions of Rex's deceitfulness performing inside her head, Marlie barely kept the sneer from her voice. "I'm gratified that I meet with your approval. As for taking you up on your suggested lodging tonight, I'll have to ask Ryan. He was looking forward to one last night in a motel bed."

The smile dropped from the man's face as if it had been scraped off with a sharp garden tool. "You're not alone?"

"No, I'm . . ." Marlie's words drifted off as she glanced over the man's shoulder. Just as she was feeling relieved that her deception was going to work, Ryan had to show up and spoil everything. To make matters worse, he was acting his juvenile self. She winced at his appearance. "...with him," she finished lamely, motioning to the boy.

Ryan, how could you? she silently groaned. The child was decked out in a costume she witnessed in only one situation—when he felt threatened by male competition. Ryan's odd apparel consisted of an old Halloween Dracula cape, a black football helmet and a pair of sunglasses. He called this getup his Barf Dater Eliminator uniform, which not only explained Ryan's purpose, but gave fair warning to any offenders.

Oh well, she thought, stifling a wayward bubble of laughter. Maybe this would solve her problem.

It did. Better than she could have imagined.

When she looked back at the man, she had expected at least a wry smile, but she didn't get one. His earlier grim countenance had been mere practice for this one as he stared at Ryan endlessly. Finally, apparently unable to stand the sight of the child a moment longer, he closed the hood of the truck with unwarranted force, turned on his cleated heel and strode toward his car.

Well, this certainly was a new reaction to Ryan's antics. As needful as it had been to end their fruitless tête-à-tête, Marlie hadn't meant to frighten the man, for he had been helpful. "Hey," she called in a jovial voice, "the kid's not really dangerous." No response. "Can I at least ask the name of the man I should thank?" she yelled more loudly.

The man faced her as he flung open his car door. "Powell. Bryce Powell," he answered curtly. "But you can save your thanks." He slid into the seat and slammed the door.

Lethargy seeped into Marlie's muscles, leaving her motionless in a wake of sudden emotional destruction. Her mind refused to assemble any coherent thought, but created an insensible vacuum that pulled her deeper within herself. That blessed escape may have lasted an eternity if not for the call of one small voice that could penetrate the profound emptiness.

"Aunt Marlie?"

She turned slowly to Ryan, then experienced a rush of returned feelings. Until this moment she hadn't realized how much she dreaded meeting Ryan's parents. Was this reaction a dismal preface to their pending relationship? It couldn't be. But the ambivalence of enemy and friend prevailed, assimilating itself in a fear and confusion as strong as Rex Kane had ever inspired.

"Get into the truck, Ryan," she commanded him brusquely.

"But, Aunt Marlie—"

"Get into the truck! Please," she said more calmly, seeing the bewildered hurt on the child's face. "It's time to go."

With flapping cape and intelligible grumbling, Ryan did as he was told. Marlie followed, steadfastly ignoring the maroon Saab parked behind her. Once seated behind the wheel, she noticed the tools she still held in her hand. His tools. She dropped them as if they were venomous serpents.

"What's the matter, Aunt Marlie?" Ryan asked, his distress unmistakable.

Marlie mentally shook herself, trying to deny the panic that was a lit stick of dynamite tied to her composure. If she didn't get out of this alley in the next few seconds she would explode. "Nothing, darling," she said soothingly. "That nice man fixed our truck. Everything is just fine now."

Barf Dater Eliminator was on the job, defending his beloved Aunt Marlie against all injustices. "That guy wasn't nice. He was rude to you," he declared belligerently. Then slyly he added, "But I fixed him, Aunt Marlie. While he wasn't looking, I took the wind out of two of his sails for you."

Marlie stared numbly at her nephew, not knowing whether to laugh or cry. To give expression to either would certainly be inviting hysteria. For if she wasn't mistaken— and with Ryan she seldom was—the darling child had just confessed to letting the air out of two of his father's tires.

Knowing why Bryce Powell would be unavoidably detained in the alley, Marlie wasted no time in vacating the scene of Ryan's little indiscretion. She, Ryan and Happy Hanson's pickup continued on their bumpy course, and thank goodness, made it to the apartment complex before Connie and Dennis could have another parting of the ways.

By the time Marlie and Ryan entered the manager's office, Marlie had herself under control, her priorities and objectives well in hand. With Rex's threats snapping at her heels, she couldn't afford to take time out to swoon, regardless of how appealing oblivion sounded.

The manager's office compared in size and elegance to one of Stynhearst Industries broom closets. A stout woman in her late fifties reigned over a battered desk and was presently engrossed in the jigsaw puzzle spread before her.

"Mrs. Cobb?" Marlie ventured. The woman looked up. Marlie felt strangely absorbed into the gaze of warm brown eyes that reminded her of Nanny Jane's.

"Yes?"

Marlie spoke to the compelling eyes. "I was told you had an apartment for rent. We'll be here several weeks. I'm willing to pay you extra for the inconvenience of a short lease."

Mrs. Cobb got up, walked to the front of her desk and leaned against it, crossing her arms. She did her best to avoid looking at Ryan, as if the child might influence her business acumen. "I generally require at least a one-year lease, with deposits," she told the younger woman.

Marlie sighed. She had to have the *only* apartment in town, didn't she? "I'll pay you six months' rent, in cash, in advance."

Mrs. Cobb's eyebrows did an amazing volt to her graying hairline. "Who told you I had an apartment to rent?" she inquired with a trace of suspiciousness.

Marlie didn't blame the woman for wondering, but neither did she wish to answer. With little choice, she did. "Bryce Powell."

The mention of his name cleared the murky atmosphere like a spring shower. Mrs. Cobb literally beamed at Marlie—and at Ryan." Oh, well," the landlady exclaimed. "If Bryce recommends you, there's no question that you and your son will stay with me while you're in Sunnydale."

Marlie gulped. Mr. Powell hadn't exactly recommended her. Did she have to be *that* honest? Not unless Mrs. Cobb asked, she decided. She could, however, straighten out the woman on the subject of hers and Ryan's relationship. "Mrs. Cobb, I'd like you to meet my nephew, Ryan." She nudged him forward, and he shyly took the lady's hand.

"Hello, Ryan. There are several children about your age in this complex and they all seem to gather in my kitchen for homemade cookies about once a day. My apartment is over this office. We'd be pleased if you'd join us." Her offer came with the benign enthusiasm of a mother with an empty nest.

Ryan turned wide eyes on Marlie, silently asking if this lady was for real. She smiled noncommittally at the woman, for until she knew just how friendly Sunnydale was, she couldn't entrust Ryan's safety with anyone.

Mrs. Cobb didn't notice that she hadn't received an answer as she busily extracted the correct forms from a filing cabinet across the room. She returned and presented Marlie with an ink pen and a contract. Before Marlie could take them, the landlady jerked them back, a blush staining her cheeks. "Would you like to see the apartment first?"

Marlie shook her head. What was the point of looking over the only apartment in town? She signed the lease, then withdrew the appropriate funds in hundred-dollar bills from her purse. Her cash didn't faze the landlady, but apparently Marlie's signature did. Mrs. Cobb stared at the name on the dotted line a moment, then looked at Marlie, plainly trying to recollect the significance of either. Suddenly the woman's eyes widened slightly, and Marlie knew the lady was remembering where she'd come across the name Marlena Stynhearst.

Fear zinged along Marlie's nerve endings, stinging the tips of her fingers and toes, robbing her of breath. Rex Kane had been here in Sunnydale. Was he still here? Was he perhaps staying in this very complex?

Marlie feigned a laugh and selected what she hoped was a likely response. "I know what you're thinking, Mrs. Cobb," she intoned lightly. "I suspect a man was here not long ago, asking about a Marlena Stynhearst."

The landlady pouted her bottom lip. "I don't have a very good poker face, do I? He wanted to surprise you. He left a number for me to call if you showed up."

"Don't you worry, Mrs. Cobb." Marlie comforted her, with her own heart pounding in anything but comfort. "I crossed paths with the man recently, and he managed a big surprise." She pursed her lips, then asked brightly, "I forgot to ask him if he was coming back through Sunnydale, though. Did he mention anything to you?"

"He said he'd drop by to check again. That was a couple of weeks ago. He was a nice-looking man," she allowed with a hint of genial busybodiness. "Is he a business associate?"

"We work at the same Los Angeles firm, but we're on different missions that just happened to be on a possible collision course, this time," she answered.

"Well, I'm glad things worked out," Mrs. Cobb said, grabbing a set of keys from the pegboard behind her desk. "I'd hate to spoil someone's surprise."

Marlie surreptitiously sighed with relief. Rex had left Sunnydale and wouldn't return for a while. She'd bought precious time with that circuitous route across the country, but she didn't hold out much hope that Rex would give up the search for his missing victims indefinitely. After all, she had snatched his little ace in the hole from under his nose, and she had possession of a tape that would send him up the river on a very long trip. In a day or two she would have to take steps to secure more time in Sunnydale. For now, she was satisfied that Rex wasn't residing under any nearby rocks.

Marlie hadn't quite recovered from her jubilation over the outcome of this disturbing conversation with Mrs. Cobb before Mrs. Cobb was introducing another disturbing topic.

Until the landlady mentioned Bryce Powell's name again as they traversed the complex parking lot, Marlie had failed to wonder why he would know about the only vacant apartment in Sunnydale. It didn't take her long to find out. Mrs. Cobb set about informing her new tenant of every illustrious virtue characterized by Mr. Bryce Powell, another tenant.

"This will be just perfect for you, dear," Mrs. Cobb was saying. "Bryce can be a very handy man for a single woman to have around." She emitted a roguish giggle, then resumed her blithe commentary, unmindful of her companion's stoic interest. She jiggled the key in the lock, opened the door and led the parade inside, all without breaking her verbal stride.

Marlie wanted to drop a trash can over this blazing torch of information and demand the answer to one pertinent question: What about Mrs. Powell? Wasn't the lady notable enough to rate even a modest compliment? And what, for Pete's sake, was a nice woman like Mrs. Cobb doing putting a married man's services onto a public auction block?

Suddenly Marlie's jaw dropped open as a host of belated questions and speculations bombarded her. That cad in the alley, that consummation of unabashed male gall, who turned out to be Janette Powell's husband and Ryan's father, had *flirted* with her. Into what kind of family environment was she expected to leave Ryan?

Swallowing her indignation as if it were a Grand Canyon boulder, she interrupted Mrs. Cobb to ask coolly, "And how is Janette Powell doing these days?"

Marlie's question worked better than a smothering trash can; the blazing torch of information fizzled to an incredulous sputter. "Janette? Why...why Janette isn't doing too well at all, Ms. Stynhearst. She's been dead for almost two years."

# Two

Bryce Powell—a thirty-four-year-old self-professed failure, but with great potential for improvement—stared vacantly out his windshield at the alley's endless expanse of potholes. He felt as he had just been clubbed over the head, dumped into one of those potholes and left for the vultures to pick clean his bones.

Happy Hanson's pickup and its two rental occupants had rattled on down the alley long ago. Soon, Bryce would have to get up the energy—or the nerve—to follow them. He didn't want to. Or maybe he did. At the moment, he wasn't too certain what was going on inside his head.

The past few months, Bryce had worked with an honest faith in success to smooth out all the wrinkles in his life. Then that woman had to come along, all bright-eyed and sassy-tongued, and towing along the one thing guaranteed to wad him up again.

Why couldn't she have been alone? Why did she have to have that fresh batch of unnerving wrinkles tagging along with her?

Bryce slammed the heel of his hand into the dash and felt the tremor clear to his brain. Good. Maybe it would shake things back into place and he wouldn't feel like going home to a bottle of spiritual consoler and celebrating his backslide into self-pity. Maybe he wouldn't be tempted to close his eyes and see again that pugnacious little rascal who had joined the woman in front of Happy Hanson's pickup. And maybe he wouldn't feel like the coward he was for walking off and leaving them puzzled by his rude behavior. The alternative would have been worse, of course. Watching a grown man shattered into a million pieces at the sight of a little boy would fluster the most unflappable.

Why wouldn't the anguish of losing his own son leave him? Bryce wondered angrily. It had been four and a half years, for heaven's sake. Almost half a decade had passed, and yet the pain still twisted in his gut from a festering wound that refused to heal.

If his son had died, perhaps Bryce and his Janette could have eventually buried the torment with their son's tiny body. But little Gordon hadn't been found dead. He hadn't been found at all. During the span of five minutes, someone had crept into their backyard and taken their eighteen-month-old son from his patio swing. The unfathomable cruelty executed in those fleeting moments had taken more from Bryce than he feared he could ever replace.

The authorities, volunteers and hired professionals, along with himself and Janette, had launched a nationwide search for Gordon. No stone was left unturned. No expense was spared. He and Janette faced financial ruin in their quest to recover their stolen child, but it hadn't been enough. In the end, after exhausting every possibility, the searchers had shaken their heads and declared the child beyond their reach.

When it was over, Bryce had lain in bed night after night, with horror stories of missing children augmenting his imagination, torturing him with visions of Gordon's probable fate. He had known that Janette lay beside him, sharing that agony, but he had been helpless to comfort her, for there had been no comfort for himself.

Painful months passed before Bryce could face acceptance of the awful truth that his son was gone. With that need to accept came a fragile hope of rallying their spirits and getting on with their lives.

Maybe that would have happened had he and Janette been given more time.

It was still difficult for Bryce to think of Janette as dead. To him, it was more like she was missing in action. Sometimes, shamefully, he was angry at her for deserting him the way she had. She should have stayed and helped him through the crushing disappointment, through the haunting dreams and shattering realities, as he had wanted to help her. People who loved each other clung to remnants of hope and together built a new future. But Janette had left him, though God knows, he didn't truly believe she wanted to. Still, she had gone to an infinite peace and left him alone to battle the demons of living.

For what seemed an eternity after her death, the demons were winning that battle. Gordon's kidnapping, Janette's death and a financially devastated air-freight company finally brought the stalwart Bryce Powell to his knees. Life had defeated him.

By day, he had buried himself in work that accomplished nothing. By night, he found solace in a bottle and the arms of an occasional woman who looked as if she could pass through his life without rousing his stymied emotions. One by one, his friends and family helplessly backed away from the frightening apparition of the man he had once been.

Then, almost a year ago, a miracle from heaven fell into his lap. The relief brought by the occasion was so immense that Bryce could actually smile at the incident now. He had been on one of his weekend self-indulgences when he woke up to find himself alone in a strange house, in a strange neighborhood somewhere in Hartford. Bemused, he had walked the streets looking for his misplaced car when he happened upon an old man who would change Bryce's life forever. Arthur Newton had said the words that finally dragged Bryce out of his apathetic haze.

Old Art had a knack for helping a man sift through the ashes of his life, showing him what was worth salvaging, what could be restored, and what should be tossed away as useless rubble. During the past months, Bryce had returned to Art's modest home to collect more of the kind man's wisdom. And lately, Bryce found himself passing on the advice at opportune moments.

These days Bryce felt as if he was a man finally healing from a long, catastrophic illness. He still had tender spots, and at times he grew weary under the strain of memories. But he was healing.

Acknowledging his fragile confidence in affairs of the heart, Bryce thought he'd found exactly what he could handle stalled in Happy Hanson's pickup. The lady's sunny disposition and whimsical sense of humor had lit up the dark corners of his heart, making her irresistible to man a who had been too long without a reason to smile.

Sunny. He didn't even know her name, but Sunny would do. Everything about her glowed. Her peachy skin, the gold and auburn highlights in her hair, the smile on her lips or the one in her eyes, all created an effect that warmed him in more ways than one. Yeah, he could have used a few nights of basking in the warmth of that petite, curving body and its dazzling accessories.

And the best thing about Sunny? She was transient. Her few weeks stay in Sunnydale wouldn't have been long enough to tempt him with an attachment that he wasn't ready to accept.

Bryce sighed with elaborate wistfulness. Sunny visiting Sunnydale—it had an almost portentous ring to it. Almost. All his great expectations had gone awry when he met her little caped traveling companion. Knowing he was being rude, hating his weakness, Bryce had, nevertheless, turned around and walked away. As much as he would have enjoyed pursuing a relationship with the woman, the child left the idea dead in his mind.

*That's what you deserve for getting your hopes up, idiot.* He mentally lambasted himself. *What goes up must come down.* He knew that was defeatist talk; Art Newton would shake a shaming finger at him for such thought language. Yet what else— *Honk! Honk! Honk!*

Bryce's eyes darted to the rearview mirror in a flash of annoyance. A black-and-white police car had pulled within a yard of his bumper. Grinning, he opened his door and walked over to the only law enforcement Sunnydale employed. Bracing his arms against the car door, Bryce revived his withering irritation for the sake of an old friendship. "Nickolas Vaughn, what the heck is an obvious waste of the taxpayers' money like you doing harassing a Sunnydale citizen?"

The six-foot-four-inch ex-New York police detective stuck his strikingly handsome head out the window and growled, "Bryce Powell, you couldn't catch an easy pop-fly using a bathtub for a baseball mitt, but you could catch thirty days for insulting a police officer." He motioned to the Saab. "And for illegal parking, too, runt."

Bryce smiled. "How you do go on about one lousy inch, pretty boy. I was just getting ready to move on. Had a little trouble in the alley a few minutes ago."

"Uh-huh. I saw the trouble you were having as she pulled out the other end of the alley in Happy Hanson's truck. Darn Ellie Jamison's timing. If she'd looked out her kitchen window a little sooner and reported that she thought Hap was stalled in the alley, I would've got to handle all that trouble myself."

Bryce put a hand on Nick's arm. "I spared you, Officer Vaughn, believe me," he said solemnly.

"Always thinking of others," Nick said dryly. "Well, do you want a lift to Jake's Garage or should I radio for a tow truck?"

"Why would I want either?" Bryce asked, puzzled.

Nick snickered and pointed at the Saab's left rear tire. Bryce swung his gaze in that direction, then muttered one word of the barnyard variety that summed up the situation nicely.

"Better make that a double, Bryce," Nick said, laughing, "for your trouble has come in pairs." He motioned to have a look at the other rear tire.

Already resigned to what he'd find, Bryce walked between the cars, looked, and made it a double. Unless Sunny had the talents of Houdini, there was but one person who could have sneaked back here and let the air out from his tires. Nick was right; trouble came in pairs—in varied shapes, sizes and ages.

Soundlessly, Bryce emitted a groan that came from the depths of his soul. Hadn't he been clever to point all that tribulation in the direction of his very own front door?

Veronica Cobb, Sunnydale's only landlady, was a good-natured woman who pretended to overlook a *faux pas* committed by society's ignorant. Marlie knew this because the dear lady had quickly dismissed Marlie's mortifying foolishness in inquiring about the health of a deceased woman.

Even now, twenty minutes after Mrs. Cobb had left the apartment, Marlie felt numbed by the news of Janette Powell's death. Mrs. Cobb had babbled several commiserating comments of the tragedy in poor Bryce Powell's life. Yes, Marlie agreed that losing a wife and a child would be tragic. She had lost her family, though perhaps the true tragedy had been the absence of grief of the lone survivor.

To truly empathize with Bryce Powell's circumstances, she had to think of losing the one dearest to her—Ryan. The results of this emotional exercise did nothing but create a conflict between acknowledging Mr. Powell's understandable anguish and sympathizing with her own persecutor.

At best, Marlie's position in this mess was terrible. She'd been counting on a female presence to which she could emotionally connect, for a woman would have better understood the vital importance of a child in one's life. With Janette Powell gone, Marlie was left to deal with not only a childless father but a mourning widower.

Or was she? Mrs. Cobb said Janette had died two years ago. Did inconsolable grief linger this long? Marlie replayed the scene in the alley, picturing the ruggedly handsome Bryce Powell. He had been alternately flirty and churlish. Were these stages of grief? She didn't know. What she did know was that she was being forced to befriend an unpredictable male, and thanks to her nephew's naughty gallantry in the alley, she had to start out that relationship with an apology.

*What would you do, Nanny Jane?* Marlie whispered to her departed friend and mentor. But Marlie knew what she would say: Do the right thing, Marlena. Do the right thing.

Marlie squeezed her eyes shut, fisted her sweaty palms and mentally rehearsed the upcoming interview with Ryan's parent. Ugh! was what she thought of the results. It wasn't very eloquent, but comprehensive and probably prophetic.

"What's the matter, Aunt Marlie? Don't you like our new apartment?"

Her eyes popped open and the fuzzy visage of her nephew dominated her view as he pressed his nose to hers. She pulled back a few inches and glanced at Ryan's attire. Thankfully, he had retired his uniform, which was absolutely necessary for the evening's remaining dubious entertainment.

"Ryan—" she began sternly.

"Not exactly our penthouse in L.A., though, is it?" The boy chattered on evasively.

"Ryan—"

"But the walls have fresh paint and the carpets are clean, aren't they? The curtains look swell. Where's the cook and the housekeeper? Are we sleeping on the floor, tonight?"

Marlie grabbed the conversation floor while Ryan took a breath. "Ryan," she commanded. "Zip it!"

Ryan knew her tone and obeyed.

Marlie took a deep breath and straightened the discouraged slump of her shoulders. "First, in brief response to your questions and excellent observations of this apartment, yes, yes, I agree, we won't have either, and probably."

The boy let out a whoop of approval, raising his fists above his head. *"Al-l ri-ight!"*

"Grab some pleasure while you can, kid. Before we camp out tonight, you are going to apologize to that man who was in the alley."

"What for?" he asked innocently.

"For taking the wind out of two of his sails. I'm on to you, Ryan B. Stynhearst. You let the air out of his tires, didn't you?"

"Yes."

For once, Marlie wished she hadn't raised the child to be so scrupulously honest. "Let's go," she ordered wearily.

"Ah, Aunt Marlie," he complained, screwing up his face in one of those scowls she didn't trust.

"Don't 'ah, Aunt Marlie' me. I'm not looking forward to facing that man again, either. I'd send you over there alone if I didn't fear he'd send back your individual body parts in little plastic bags." The prospect of physical violence amused Ryan. It didn't amuse Marlie, for she wasn't positive that she was joshing him.

According to the informative Mrs. Cobb, Bryce Powell occupied the town house two doors down. Ryan dragged his feet and Marlie dragged her spirits, but eventually the few yards separating the red brick town houses were covered. She rang the doorbell several times, then deciding that Mr. Powell must not have had enough time to change two tires, turned to leave.

Two steps down the sidewalk, she heard the door behind her burst open. She glanced over her shoulder and what she saw filling the portal described best as a modern day version of an Avenging Angel. A near-naked Avenging Angel. Bryce Powell hadn't shaved or bathed yet, but he'd removed his shoes, socks and sweaty ball jersey, and had left his pants hitched low on his hips.

All that bronzed, hair-roughened flesh might have impressed a woman who went in for that sort of thing, but at the moment Marlie was more entranced by the look in his eyes. It wasn't pleasant. Her skin prickled painfully from the darts of wrath being tossed her way by Bryce Powell's lethal gaze. Embarrassment and apprehension crowded in on her at once, making it impossible to decide how to respond to such blatant hostility.

Ryan, bless his intrepid nature, took the problem out of her hands—temporarily. "Aunt Marlie says I have to apologize to you," he told the tall, scowling man. "I will, but I'm not really sorry."

"Ryan!"

The child guilelessly looked up at his aunt. "Did you want me to lie to him?"

Yes. Yes! she silently screamed. I'm fighting to keep my life afloat and you're tossing me cement blocks. She sneaked a peak at Ryan's father—Ryan's father...that took some getting used to—and was surprised to find him lounging in his doorway, an eyebrow arrogantly cocked. No doubt he was waiting to see how she would handle this rebellion.

Frankly, she didn't have the foggiest idea of what to do about it. Except for a frightening streak of curiosity and an intolerance for intruding men, which was an attitude Marlie had come to respect, Ryan was the picture of a perfect child. How could she possibly discipline him for his honesty?

Deciding to take the bull by the horns, she grasped the smaller beast by the ear and propelled him beneath the nose of the larger. "Mr. Powell," she said gravely, "this is Ryan. As you've undoubtedly guessed, he's responsible for your delay in getting home. He *is* sorry for causing you this inconvenience, he just doesn't know it yet. But," she looked at Ryan, her meaning explicit, "he will when I get him back home."

Ryan held his ground, his furrowed brow and narrowed eyes telling Marlie that he'd take anything she dished out, but he would not be sorry. Marlie sighed and turned back to the glaring man. "Ryan sees himself as my protector," she explained ruefully.

An inexplicable expression crossed Mr. Powell's face when he glanced down at Ryan. Emotion churned the muscles of his clinched jaw until he finally dragged his eyes back to her. A steely moment passed, then the arrogant eyebrow hiked again. "And just what does the little brat think he's protecting you from?"

It took about two seconds for Mr. Powell's word choice to sink in and hit a nerve. Brat? Brat! Marlie's green eyes glittered dangerously, like shards of a broken wine bottle. Compassion and aspiring friendship fell through a trapdoor in her mind, and the stage was instantly reset for a battle scene. *Nobody* insulted her pride and joy. She met Mr. Powell's eyes with penetrating coldness and said, "From brutish men like you."

Bryce shouldered away from the doorjamb and assumed the stance of a man just itching for a good verbal tussle with a woman. "Let's back up and review the incident, lady. *I* was the victim in that alley."

From somewhere inside her, a sensible Marlie was desperately trying to coach the Marlie who wanted to kick this bully in the shin. *Friendship. Remember the objective is friendship. You* must *impress this man.*

Shoot. How she hated giving up the fight just as she was finding the courage to take on something as intimidating as the man looming over her. To surrender was reminiscent of that ugly corner Rex had backed her into only a month ago. But for the sake of the greater scheme of things, she bowed to her sensibility, hoping to do a little impressing along the way.

"Yes, you were a victim, Mr. Powell," she concurred in a voice of reason. "But not before I was. I've taught Ryan courtesy and respect. Blaring away at me with your car horn was a perfect example of rudeness. He thought I should be championed and did it the only way he knew how."

Bryce stepped out of the doorway, subtly moving in on his prey. As right as the woman was about his manners, he couldn't back off and graciously accept an apology now if his life had depended on it. That would end this encounter.

The little boy had sneaked off, and without that bittersweet hardship to endure, Bryce felt freer to pursue the pleasure at hand. Honestly, he'd hoped once he was away from this woman his initial response to her would settle into a sensible perspective and he'd forget her. But no such luck. On the contrary, she made him feel like a schoolboy again, complete with raging hormones and a downright placid intellect.

This scintillating interlude couldn't last forever, though. The child would show up again and blow a ragged hole in his desire. Until that time, Bryce could take advantage of what was available.

"Your son's sense of justice is positively frightening," he said, grinning wryly as he eased an advance along the sidewalk. "If my social infraction had been more severe, would he have slashed my tires rather than just let the air out?"

Marlie gritted her teeth. For each step he prowled forward, she measured the same distance backward. Her hopes for a mutually advantageous relationship with the man were progressing the same way. She'd reached the end of his sidewalk and retrenched behind a handy, waist-high yew a sidestep away. "Mr. Powell," she said wearily, suffering from faltering morale, "Ryan is not my son, but I've done my best as his guardian for three years."

Bryce smiled nastily. "Then perhaps his delinquent tendency is a heredity flaw, and you can find comfort in blaming the poor father."

A funny little hiccup erupted from Marlie's throat as she tried to swallow a hoot of laughter. If Mr. Powell only knew how credible his conjecture was.

With a puzzled smile, he edged around the side of the bush asking, "I said something funny?"

"Sort of," she admitted merrily, carefully maintaining a diagonal position from him. That she was being stalked wasn't lost to her, but his bush was wide and his dimples were cute, and the lightened mood was quickly reclaiming a lot of lost territory. "Will you forgive Ryan for his overzealous defenses of a favorite aunt?" she asked.

Bryce pretended to ponder her question, at the same time attempting to close the space separating them. It didn't work; she matched him inch for inch. And he was *tired* of beating around this bush. Thankful for long arms, he simply reached across the yew and snagged the woman's shoulders, whereupon reeling her in was like fighting a feisty trout.

Finally he had her where he wanted her, but she had pokered up on him. The expression on her face was empty, or perhaps frightened. "Hey, don't lose it, Sunny," he said gently. "I was just going to suggest a kiss in lieu of an apology?"

While blindly struggling, Marlie had felt only Rex's hands controlling her, remembered only her humiliating frailty yielding to his strength. But this calm, gentle voice didn't belong to Rex. Her eyes swept the length of his bare chest and upward. The smiling mouth, the enticing dimples, the intense blue eyes were not Rex's, either. "I . . . I think if you want to kiss and make up with Ryan, that would be fine."

Bryce slowly shook his head. "Not the kid. You."

Marlie's gaze fell to his bare feet. "I didn't let the air out of your tires," she murmured.

"But someone has to make retribution, and the kid's gone. So how about it?"

Her head snapped up. "Gone? Where—?" In that instant, a little black tornado tore around the yew, dodged her legs and seized her captor just above the knees. Caught unaware, Mr. Powell went down hard and fast and became buried from the belly up beneath a swirl of sateen cape.

"You leave my Aunt Marlie alone," Barf Dater Eliminator yelled. His fists were clinched, but he needed them to manage his wobbly headgear.

Marlie stuck her own fist in her mouth to hold back a wail of alarm. With eyes rounded fearfully, she watched Mr. Powell pluck the small nuisance from his chest as he bounded to his feet. He stood Ryan beside Marlie, gave her another one of his infamous scowls and promised grimly, "Later."

He stalked off toward his front door. Marlie grabbed Ryan's hand and made tracks to her own. Glad now that she'd left the door ajar for a quick escape, she shoved Ryan into the foyer. As she crossed the threshold herself, she caught a glimpse of Mr. Powell ferociously frowning her way as he leaned a naked shoulder against his closed front door. "Oh, no," she moaned, turning to Ryan. "Did you lock Mr. Powell out of his apartment?" she demanded of the grinning boy.

"Yes."

Marlie rolled her eyes heavenward. "Please, give me strength," she muttered. She slammed the front door, scolded Ryan for his devilish behavior and capped the punishment with a denied treat: no sleeping on the floor tonight. Ryan was disheartened, but not subdued. Marlie feared she hadn't seen the end of the Eliminator.

Ready to see through her threat of providing sensible sleeping provisions, she and Ryan, in Happy Hanson's reluctant transport, made a trip downtown, circumventing that dreadful alley. Connie, Dennis and the rest of the gang under the truck hood behaved while her excursion took her to a store for household accessories, a store for food and cleaning supplies and last, a furniture store. She paid cash for an entire houseful of furnishings, then stared in disbelief at the owner when he informed her it was too late to expect delivery tonight.

Marlie had never punched a time clock, but she suspected her heart wouldn't stop if she failed to punch out at five o'clock sharp. Wryly, she asked the owner if his time-sensitive employees might manage to toss her two mattresses into the truckbed. Obsequiously, he assured his customer that they could, and promised delivery of the rest of her order tomorrow.

Once back at their town house, Marlie realized her ordeal wasn't over. How was she going to get two mattresses out of the truck and up a flight of stairs? Five minutes into a wrestling match with the first mattress, which left her pinned with a smashed face to the truck rails she knew she wasn't. Not without bigger help than little Ryan.

Bigger help arrived. The mattress was plucked off her body like a speck of lint. Glancing down, Marlie recognized the bare feet of her rescuer and wondered painfully why she was shown at her worst advantage every time they crossed paths.

"Thank you, Mr. Powell," she called morosely from her side of the mattress.

"Bryce. And you're welcome," he barked back. Then he muttered, "You don't know how welcome you'd be under different circumstances."

Marlie heard his words, but didn't understand them. She didn't think she wanted to, given the wide range of possible interpretations. "Can I help you with the mattresses?" she asked tentatively.

"No."

And indeed she would have been superfluous to the task. Bryce lugged each mattress up the stairs while Marlie kept Ryan out of his way. Bryce might have appreciated her consideration, as well he should, but she couldn't be certain. The taciturn man looked at neither she nor Ryan.

The job done, her reluctant knight vanished from the premises in dramatic silence. Marlie didn't bother thanking him a second time.

Not wanting to give too much of her financial position away, Marlie opted to do her own cooking and cleaning.

This turned out to be an adventure in domestic horror. Ryan begged to help, which made two bungling housekeepers, but somehow things shaped up, with only minor calamities marking the passage of their ineptitude.

By then, the sun rested on the Sunnydale rooftops. Marlie had promised Mr. Hanson the return of his truck before dark, so after a light super, she loaded up Ryan and bounced across town to Mr. Hanson's produce corner. Happy appeared pleased to see his piece of junk home safe and sound. Chuckling to herself, Marlie surmised that this optimistic attitude was what had earned the man his name.

Thirty minutes later, Marlie and Ryan entered on foot what she'd christened Pothole Alley. It was dusk and the sporadically placed streetlights cast a gloomy pallor over the scene. Ryan, who never missed a thing no matter what the visibility, found a poor dead cat in the tall grass beside the pavement.

"I bet Mr. Powell hit him with his car," he observed implacably.

"Ryan, that's an unfair thing to say," she replied firmly, but with inward uncertain confidence.

"I still bet he did. Look how flat this kitty is. From the decomposition, I'd say Mr. Powell hit him a couple of weeks ago, and he didn't even stop to bury him."

"The sanitation department usually takes care of animal hit-and-runs, Ryan. Maybe Mr.—" She halted, realizing that she was halfway agreeing with Ryan's theory. Before she could correct that impression, headlights cut through the murky darkness. She pulled Ryan to one side of the alley to allow the vehicle by, but the vehicle stopped beside them.

Fear had no more than started percolating through her system when she recognized the maroon Saab. The passenger window descended. Bryce Powell's voice hit the warm night air like dry ice. "Get into the car."

A hundred suggestions of what he could do with his offered ride rampaged through Marlie's mind. Unfortunately, she couldn't afford the luxury of expressing any of them. She started to put Ryan in the front seat, but Mr. Powell put a stop to that notion.

"You in the front. The kid in the back. And if he pulls one trick, I'll stop the car and lash him to the bumper."

Marlie complied. And seethed. And prayed that Ryan possessed enough self-preservation to take this man at his word. She slammed her car door, pressed tightly against it and waited for the next decree to be passed down.

What came next was more on the order of an inquisition.

"What's your name?" Bryce snapped out.

"Marlie Stynhearst."

"Where are you from?"

"Los Angeles."

"Do you often take walks through dark alleys in Los Angeles?"

"No more often than I allow a strange man to order me into his car."

That shut him up. The twenty remaining potholes took a million years to traverse, but finally they reached the complex parking lot. Bryce pulled into her slot and cut the engine. Marlie didn't know what to say; "thank you" hadn't worked worth a darn in the past, so she shrugged and grasped the door handle. Mr. Powell's hand on her arm stopped her.

"I'd like to talk to you, Marlie. Privately."

Talk? Yes, they needed to talk. But this man who suffered chronic boorishness inspired such an awesome resentment in Marlie that she didn't think she could manage a conversation without wrapping her hands around his throat. She sighed, knowing she'd have to try.

Ryan reluctantly agreed to sit on the front step of their town house when she promised to be only a minute. With the child out of earshot, she turned to her obnoxious chauffeur and couldn't resist pleasantly asking, "Are you always a jerk, or is it a latent condition triggered by the presence of civility?"

For a moment, Bryce didn't know what to say; he'd never been called a jerk to his face before. Even during his bouts with the bottle, he hadn't been a mean drunk, just a pathetic one.

After his experience with the boy this afternoon, he swore to himself he'd cut a wide path around such obvious heartache. Sweet mercy, the child looked just as he imagined his Gordon would have, had he lived. The boy, Ryan, had big blue eyes, blond curly hair and a pair of dimples that would knock the girls' socks off someday. His Gordon would have, too.

But Bryce hadn't cut a wide path around anything all afternoon except his own common sense. He'd monitored the woman's activities, then butted in whenever he saw a chance. Now he was sitting in his own car, taking insults off her because, dammit, he deserved them.

"I am not a jerk, Marlie," he said irritably. "I happen to be attracted to you."

She jumped on that. A gasp prefaced her infuriated query. "You mean to tell me you've been snorting and stomping around all afternoon because you're... you're...?"

Bryce blinked in surprise. It took no imagination to fill in the blanks of her accusation. Well, well, Ms. Stynhearst, he thought, delighted with her giant leap at a wild conclusion. Even he hadn't quite narrowed down his anxieties to that indelicate distinction. But yes, sexual frustration was an acceptable excuse for his behavior. Better than admitting that he wanted her, but that her kid broke his heart.

"Yes, Marlie Stynhearst," he said matter-of-factly. "I am. So unless you're interested in going to bed with me, we have nothing else to say." He paused, then asked, "So, what do you say?"

Total silence reigned in the dark interior of the Saab. At length, Bryce nodded. "That's what I thought you'd say." He reached across her lap and released the door handle. "Goodbye, Sunny. It's been hellish knowing you."

After slamming the door with enough force to rock the Saab on its axles, Marlie stomped up her sidewalk, ordered Ryan to his feet, then applied a forced entry to her front door that any burglar would applaud. The sacks of new linen waited in the foyer. She pointed to them and instructed Ryan, "Please go make up the mattresses." Ryan, again demonstrating a remarkable sensitivity toward his aunt's moods, gathered the sacks and scatted.

Marlie plopped herself down on the bottom step, where she chewed on her opinions of Mr. Powell as if they were raw meat.

Bryce Powell wasn't stricken with grief. He wasn't embittered by loss. He was a sexually deprived Neanderthal. All those barbaric rumblings she'd heard every time they'd met had been the thump of his club and the grunt of his mating call.

Now that she thought about it, she realized that Bryce Powell's entire, consuming attention had been focused on her, not on the little boy who had left him stranded in an alley, and tackled him in his front yard and locked him out of his house. Ryan undoubtedly upset him, but it was she who was the object of his roving eye.

Being single, he was free to rove an eye over any unattached female he chose—herself included, if it made him happy—just as long as he didn't expect the compliment returned. The last time she indulged in a little roving, she tripped over her own stupidity and landed in a pack of trouble.

No, her association with Bryce Powell was going to stay on a strictly...what? Impersonal basis? Impossible. She had to make friends with that man. She had to impress that man. And at the same time, she had to manage to stay out of the bushes with that man. Assuming she accomplished those small feats, she had to mediate a relationship between father and son—another small feat, considering the son had declared war on the father.

Marlie grimaced. What a nice impression she had already made by being in charge of training the little warrior the past three years. She twisted around to frown up the staircase, the direction of Ryan's activities. "You're lucky that man chooses to ignore you, kid," she muttered.

She went upstairs, prepared to find two mattresses neatly made and Ryan ready for prayers and a bedtime story from an article in *Science Digest*. That's not what she found.

A familiar bewilderment stopped her at Ryan's door as she heard again the child's chanted words coming faintly through the wooden panel.

"Born of faith, love and joy,
My child, don't be forlorn.
Play for us your song of hope,
Upon this silver horn."

A strange little rhyme, Marlie thought. Stranger still because Ryan couldn't remember where he'd heard it, though
he'd recited it numerous times in the past three years. The
rhyme had, however, established a pattern of occurring
during her nephew's most distressed moods.

Instantly concerned, Marlie pushed open the door and
entered to find Ryan huddled in a corner of the room.
"What's wrong, darling?" she asked gently, stooping beside him.

"Nothing," he muttered, though his sad little face said
"everything." Marlie smiled and drew him tightly against
her. "Well, if you were going to pick one thing that could be
wrong, what would it be?" she asked.

Ryan's eyes swept over her face, searching. "I could be
worried that you were going to leave me. But you wouldn't
leave, would you, Aunt Marlie? We're going to play ball
tomorrow, aren't we?"

Tears pierced Marlie's eyelids. How well she could relate
to Ryan's insecurities. Swallowing, much less speaking, became a Herculean task that she had to perform. "Ryan, you
can be sure if I have to go somewhere for a while, I will return to you."

"Do you promise?"

"Always," she said, and prayed that she could keep it.

Reassured, Ryan then helped Marlie prepare the mattresses and allowed himself to be tucked in for the night.
Exhausted herself, she made quick but ginger use of her
dubiously sanitized bathroom facilities, then aimed her
body at the inviting mattress on her bedroom floor.

Dreams. Horrible dreams invaded her sleep. Fractured
scenes of Ryan being wrenched from her, first by Rex, then
by Bryce Powell. *"Aunt Marlie, don't leave me,"* Ryan
cried. But it was too dark; she couldn't find him. She
reached out, but no small body came into her arms.

She was alone. Afraid.

Marlie jerked awake, trembling, tears streaming down her face. Fear sent her fleeing to Ryan's room. A dream, just a dream, she assured herself as she knelt beside his bed. Relieved, she offered up sincere thankfulness.

"Aunt Marlie, did you have a nightmare?" Ryan whispered, his hand moving consolingly over her bent head.

Marlie looked at his sweet face, radiant in the moonlight from the window. She smiled. "Yes," she whispered back, "but I'm fine now, because you're here."

"I'll take care of you, Aunt Marlie. You don't have to be afraid."

"I know." She kissed his cheek, then went back to her bed, feeling inexplicably better.

Marlie's travel alarm clock awoke her at six o'clock the next morning. Rolling off the mattress, her feet just missed tramping on a small black bundle on the floor. A closer look revealed a sleeping Ryan, in Eliminator uniform, guarding her bedside.

In that moment, Marlie knew that she would allow nothing to separate her permanently from this child. Biology, ethicality and legality may be on Bryce Powell's side, but love was on hers. Somehow she would make that point work in her favor.

# Three

Marlie, as a rule, wasn't an early riser and didn't intend to make a habit of it. But her nightmares of the night before and her not-too-successful experience with Ryan's father convinced her that today was the day to do something about gaining more time in which to improve both.

The door chimes interrupted a search through her closet for appropriate traveling apparel. She stuffed her arms into the sleeves of her silk, knee-length kimono, checked to make certain Ryan was still asleep in her bed where she'd placed him, then trotted down the stairs. Who could be calling at this hour? Assuming the worst, she took a cautious peek through the hole in the door. It wasn't Rex; maybe it was worse. Mr. Powell stood on her doorstep, looking very good in his gray pin-striped suit and red silk tie, but otherwise as grim as ever.

She opened the door and tried to smile at him. "Good morning, Mr. Powell."

"Bryce. And I disagree, Marlie." His lips twisted dourly. "My good morning fell apart when I took the garbage out."

"Oh?"

"Mmm-hmm. Imagine my dismay at finding a dead cat in my trash can."

"Ooooh."

"That wasn't exactly what I said, but I see you get my point."

Marlie slumped dejectedly against the doorjamb, unaware that her new position allowed her kimono to expose an unseemly amount of leg and chest. Bryce noticed, though. What he could see matched the mental picture of her body that he had been carrying with him since last night. He hadn't slept a wink because of it, and now his disposition felt as if it had a blister rubbed on it. "Why me?" he demanded of no one in particular.

Knowing he expected her to explain, Marlie said, "The cat in your trash can was the result of a misunderstanding. I told Ryan that the sanitation department disposes of dead animals. But the cat had been ignored, and because Ryan is a sweet, compassionate child, he took care of the problem himself."

Sweet and compassionate? Bryce stared at her a moment in disbelief, then with polite nastiness said, "You've heard the old saying, good fences make good neighbors, Marlie? If I have to, I'll build another Great Wall of China around my property to keep that sweet and compassionate nephew of yours out. If that doesn't work, I'll have to assume this is some cunning act you've devised to catch a father for the kid and a husband for yourself."

*Whap!*

Bryce rubbed his stinging cheek. Damn, but she had a fast reaction time. She had a wicked mouth on her, too, when it came to defending that kid. Her tirade meant to sting his ears, as her palm had stung his cheek. Moments passed and Marlie showed no sign of running down. Deciding to see what other wicked things her mouth could do, Bryce abruptly pulled her into his arms and terminated his verbal crucifixion with his own mouth.

Marlie struggled but he hung on, first demanding a shared desire, then sweetly cajoling her with light, playful caresses. As his kiss altered from subjugation to persuasion, so did her response. She softened and hesitantly participated in what was for him a quite pleasant event.

When the kiss ended, Bryce noted that she wasn't exactly overcome with reciprocated lust, but neither was she slapping his face again. He reluctantly let her go, not knowing whether he had won or lost this confrontation.

Marlie shared his confusion. His kiss had confounded her. She liked it; she hated it. She wanted to kiss him again to help make up her mind. She wouldn't, of course. His caress had lacked the violence she associated with Rex, but Mr. Powell had just demonstrated that he wasn't averse to using a little masculine power and an irresistible magnetism to get what he wanted.

As for his horrible accusation, it had angered her. Yes, she was trying to catch Ryan a father. But a man for herself—absolutely not! She was willing to give up a lot to keep Ryan safe, to return him to his rightful place, but she didn't feel obliged to sacrifice her self-respect. Mr. Powell had stepped over the line with his crude remark, and whether or not she had forfeited ground in their relationship with her equally crude retaliation, she refused to regret her actions. Rex's physical and emotional manipulations still doused her dignity with scalding humiliation, and she promised herself that it would be a long time before she'd submit to the dominance of another man.

She looked up into a handsome face that mirrored some curiosity, some regret and a lot of passion. The passion had to go, for practical purposes. Quietly she said, "You're off the hook, Mr. Powell. If I was looking for a husband, I wouldn't settle for an ape in a business suit."

Bryce's lips twitched with amusement. "Bryce. And I deserve the insult, along with the slap. Rest assured, three loosened jaw teeth has shown me the error of my ways." He took a step back and gave her a lopsided smile. "So long, Marlie. I'll pray that the kid doesn't turn on you in the future."

Marlie watched him go, worried. He seemed to think they were parting ways on this doorstep, but he was wrong. They would meet again, and the encounters would be complicated by an unnecessary sexual attraction. Why did he have to muddle their relationship with sex? she wondered dismally. She couldn't allow it to happen, and she wouldn't explain to him why.

Ryan came bouncing down the stairs, interrupting her rumination. He threw his sturdy little arms around her, greeted her with a perky "Good morning" and sloppy kiss on the cheek.

"I love you, Aunt Marlie," he said, sitting down beside her on the step.

Marlie sighed. "I love you, too, though I suspect you're a troublemaker."

"Am I a troublemaker?" he asked, not too disturbed by the possibility.

"Probably," she said, grinning. "I'd go broke having your motives analyzed. For instance, Mr. Powell just stopped by on his way to work. He told me about the distressing experience he had, taking out his trash this morning."

Ryan stared at his bare toes poking out the bottoms of his pajamas, but he didn't comment.

Marlie refused to talk down to Ryan. He was young but smart, and he asked questions when he didn't understand. Out of respect for his intelligence she gave it to him straight. "I'm going to choose to believe that what you did was done out of compassion for the cat," she told him gently. "If your motive was otherwise, you should be ashamed of yourself. That said, I want your promise that you will never sneak off at night again."

"Ah, Aunt Marlie, I know better than to talk to strangers, and I watched for cars."

Yes, but did you watch for Rex Kane? she wondered uneasily. "Promise me, Ryan." Her command was unyielding.

"Okay," he conceded, perturbed but resigned.

She sighed gratefully, knowing she could trust Ryan with a pinpoint precise agreement. She cuddled him closer, took a deep breath and broached a subject that she knew wouldn't thrill him any more than it did her. "Ryan, I've got some business to take care of today and I can't take you with me."

"What kind of business, Aunt Marlie? Why can't I go, too?"

"You can't go because you'd need a passport." When he was about to argue, she cut him off, explaining, "I'll be gone just for the day, I promise. If Mrs. Cobb agrees to keep you, maybe she'll let you help her make cookies." Her smile was calculated. "That'll be a new experience for you. One you won't likely get with me." It worked. Marlie watched as Ryan thought through the intriguing process of taking several ingredients and producing one product and became hooked on the idea.

Thankfully, Mrs. Cobb was, too. Marlie invested considerable anxiety over the decision to leave Ryan with a stranger, but it had to be done, and Mrs. Cobb was the best choice of unknown candidates. The landlady waved away all Marlie's apologies for the imposition and looked insulted by the offer of money. As if that wasn't enough, she refused Marlie's request to call and cancel the furniture order and instead volunteered to be on hand to supervise the delivery. With everything settled, Mrs. Cobb shooed Marlie out the door with one hand while guiding Ryan to the kitchen with the other.

It was the start of an entire mission blessed with perfection. At exactly 2:00 p.m. Marlie walked into the Bank of Winnipeg and opened a modest checking account with funds transferred from her bank in Los Angeles. As an afterthought, she went shopping, freely using her credit cards. As she was establishing herself as a new resident in the Canadian city, she knew Rex would be closely monitoring her L.A. bank account for transaction activity in hopes of locating her.

Let Rex track her here and turn Winnipeg upside down looking for her, she thought with wicked vindictiveness. Her only regret was that she wouldn't be around to watch his frustration mount.

She boarded her home-bound plane at five o'clock that evening, exhausted but elated. Hopefully, she had gained enough time to see Ryan safely settled in his rightful place, and a place for herself with him . . . if Ryan, in his unmitigated guardianship, didn't mutilate all likelihood of this happening.

Ryan's happy face flashed in her mind, and for the first time since kissing him goodbye that morning, she allowed thoughts of the child to invade her purpose. How had he and Mrs. Cobb fared? she wondered wistfully.

Actually, Mrs. Cobb and Ryan had fared wonderfully together until Mrs. Cobb received an urgent call from an ailing friend across town. It was early evening, Ms. Stynhearst wouldn't return for hours and a sickroom was no place for a little boy. What to do? Mrs. Cobb wondered frantically. Suddenly the perfect solution came to her: Bryce Powell. He could take care of an energetic little boy. Within minutes she had Ryan and his duffel bag gathered and deposited on the doorstep of the child's favorite victim.

Bryce answered the doorbell on the second ring and stared in open dismay at his visitors. Before he could oppose the invasion, his landlady had pushed the boy over his threshold and launched her persuasion speech. "Dear Bryce, thank goodness you're home. I was at my wit's end, worrying what to do with sweet little Ryan here. Mildred Smith's back is out again, poor thing, and I simply must go to her. Be a sweetheart and watch Ryan until Ms. Stynhearst returns. Ryan has the keys to their apartment if you need anything. Otherwise, I've left her a note on the door. She'll know where to look. Thanks again, you dear man. Ta ta."

And that was it. Bryce stared, slack-jawed, as the night swallowed up the perpetrator of this nightmare.

Bryce clenched his teeth against the unfairness of fate as he motioned the boy to follow. He'd put a movie in the VCR that they could both watch, then ignore the child until his aunt picked him up. With any luck, a whole evening could pass without having his heart stomped by an uncaring little squirt who had the nerve to remind Bryce too much of the joys of fatherhood that he was missing with his own son.

According to plan, Bryce filled a small bowl with popcorn and placed it, along with a cola, on the coffee table, then stretched out on the sofa with his own popcorn bowl balanced on his hip. The movie feature he chose was three hours long; if Marlie didn't come by the end of the show, he'd rewind the blasted thing and they'd watch it again.

This great plan may have worked if Ryan hadn't made plans of his own. Not the least bit interested in a dumb old war movie, he donned his uniform in the bathroom, loaded his weapon and sneaked into position. Fortuitously timed with a bombing raid on the TV screen, Ryan popped up from behind the sofa and shot Mr. Powell three times in the left ear with his water pistol. "Take that, you barf dater," he shouted triumphantly.

Bryce exploded off the sofa amid a shower of popcorn. For a stunned moment, he didn't know what had hit him. The water pistol in the hands of his weirdly dressed little visitor gave him a clue. Without giving himself time to think, he snatched the kid up and plopped him down on the kitchen bar that separated the rooms. From this level, it seemed more like talking to an adult. He spoiled the effect by growling, "How would you like a good spanking for that trick, kid?"

Ryan's chin came up and his top lip sank behind his bottom one. He looked like a tenacious little bulldog contemplating the mailman's leg. *You're going to rip my heart to shreds, aren't you, kid?* Bryce thought in morose wonder. For even while water yet dripped from his left ear, Bryce had to admire the boy's bravery.

"That's an illogical question," Ryan informed him scornfully. "No kid likes a spanking and there's no such thing as a good one, sir."

Sir? Somehow Bryce felt intimidated by the respectful title. He avoided the short, rhythmic swinging legs and disarmed the ruffian, then removed his helmet and glasses. "Illogical or not, do you get my message?" he demanded.

"Yes, sir. You don't want me to shoot you in the left ear anymore."

"Or the right ear," he added, thinking to cover all bases with this cute conniver. Then, curious despite himself, he asked, "Why do you do this to me?"

"Because you want my Aunt Marlie."

"How do you know?" he demanded incredulously. This was a kid, for Pete's sake.

"Because you look at her."

"So? Your Aunt Marlie's nice to look at."

Ryan nodded. "I know. She smells good, too."

"I wouldn't know about that. She doesn't like me to get that close."

"She does Rex."

Did Bryce truly want to know? Apparently. "Who's Rex?"

"Another barf dater. I tried to tell Aunt Marlie that he's a creep—" Ryan sighed dejectedly "—but she still engaged him."

"What do you mean, she engaged him?" Bryce asked ominously.

Ryan rolled his eyes impatiently. "They're getting married."

Bryce winced, taking an unexpected punch in the gut. "Are you sure?" he rasped.

"Well—" the boy leaned forward, anxious to confide his great secret "—the day before we left L.A. I smeared Limburger cheese on the manifold of Rex's car. That probably took care of the problem."

Bryce blanched and felt a spurt of pity for the unfortunate Rex. As for Marlie's engagement, he decided to take this news with a grain of salt. She didn't act engaged.

Heaving a great sigh, Bryce stared at the kid on his bar who could have been a clone of his own lost child. Physically, that is, he hastily amended. No child of his would have behaved like this one. "How are old you? Eight or nine?" he asked abruptly.

"Six, sir."

"You're pretty smart for a six-year-old."

"Yes, sir. I'm a genius," he said forlornly, then brightened. "But Aunt Marlie's helping me with the problem."

Bryce didn't even want to get into how Aunt Marlie could alleviate genius. He didn't doubt that she could, though, for she was certainly doing a number on *his* mental acuity. Ryan or no Ryan, he wanted Marlie in a way that seriously undermined every moral, every principle, every speck of wisdom that he professed to claim.

He defined part of his grievance as pure jealousy of a woman who had won a child by default, when he had lost his child by defeat. This tedious self-analysis wasn't improving his temper, for he was fed up with the results. Fed up with his anger and frustration and fed up with feeling like a fool for allowing a little boy to scare him away from something he wanted.

In a few weeks Marlie would be gone, and he would have missed all the good things that might have happened. He needed a dose of her spunky temperament, and he refused to be denied the pleasure of showing Marlie that she'd enjoy his company as much as he'd enjoy hers.

One way or another, the child was a fact of life to be endured, so why not make this forced confinement work in Bryce's favor? "Ryan," he said, man-to-man. "You're right about me wanting your Aunt Marlie. But I'm not like that creep, Rex, because I don't want Marlie to engage me." Not the way Ryan meant, anyway, he added mentally. "So you see, I would be a safer—" He groped for a word, which Ryan supplied.

"Barf dater?"

Bryce scowled and didn't deign to agree.

Ryan got a gleam in his eye that his Aunt Marlie would have instantly recognized. With no one around to warn this poor guy, Ryan considered him fair game. "I take you for a sporting man, sir," the boy said, giving his best salesman pitch. "So here's what I propose. A contest. If I win, you stay away from my Aunt Marlie. If you win, you can try to date her without my interference."

Bryce shook his head, marveling at the kid's temerity.

"Oh, come on, sir, I'm just a little kid. You're supposed to indulge me. Pleeease."

Bryce shrugged. Why not? The boy had to learn better sometime. "All right. Since you're just a little kid and need indulging, I'll take you up on your challenge. To make this fair, you can chose the contest."

"Video games," the child responded without hesitation.

"Okay. You have any?"

"Sure."

They trooped over to Ryan's apartment where Ryan spread out an impressive collection of games for Bryce's perusal. Bryce selected one that he had at least heard of. While Ryan raided the refrigerator, Bryce was granted a warm-up. "A piece of cake," he muttered, greatly self-assured, fifteen minutes later.

Two hours later, Bryce was sweating profusely. The kid was an outstanding player and Bryce was down ten thousand points. He saw his goal slipping through his fingers. Then he mentally pictured said goal and felt renewed determination.

Marlie entered her apartment a little after nine that night and came face-to-face with a sight that floored her—a smiling Bryce Powell standing beside a frowning Ryan. In fact, Ryan looked as if the bottom had just dropped out of his world. "What's wrong, Ryan?" she demanded, shooting an accusing glance at Mr. Powell.

"I lost you, Aunt Marlie," he said disconsolately.

Marlie swallowed heavily. With foreboding, she looked at Bryce, but asked Ryan, "How did you lose me?"

"Battling Baboons," the boy confessed, shamefaced. "Mr. Powell won, and now he gets to date you."

To say Marlie was shocked at this turn of events would have been an overdose in understatement. Ryan led his aunt to the sofa and solicitously asked if she'd like something to drink.

"Double Scotch, on the rocks," muttered a woman who had been a teetotaler all her life.

"We don't keep alcoholic beverages, Aunt Marlie," the child reminded her worriedly.

"She doesn't need booze, Ryan," Bryce interjected, a satanical smile if Marlie ever saw one twisting his lips. "She's just momentarily overcome by the joyful prospect of going out with me. It's a common reaction with the women I date."

Marlie shot him a withering glance. "I will not go out with you," she said succinctly.

"But, Aunt Marlie, you've got to," Ryan exclaimed. "I'll be a welsher, if you don't. You don't want me to be a welsher, do you?"

Bryce kept smiling. Marlie had an unholy urge to indent those dimples of his a little deeper with her fist. "It's time for you to go to bed, Ryan," she said levelly. When he would have squawked, she gave him one of her looks that sent him quietly on his way.

Alone with her prospective date, she nervously walked to the sliding doors overlooking the patio and stared into the night. Bryce allowed her to stew a few minutes, then came up behind her to wrap her loosely in his arms.

"I don't have two heads and seldom breathe real fire," he said softly. "Why is a date such a big deal?"

Marlie wanted to leap out of his tender grasp, and at the same time burrow more deeply into it. Too mixed-up to think of a sensible reason, she settled for a pitiful excuse. "It just won't work."

He gave her a little hug that brought her closer. She did smell wonderful, like spring flowers after a rain. "How do you know it won't work if you don't give it a try?"

A small, unguarded chuckle escaped. "I don't have to try sticking my elbow in my ear to know that won't work, either." She peered over her shoulder at him, her expression perplexed. "I slapped your face, for Pete's sake. Why would you want to date me?"

Bryce grinned. "Beats me. I guess I kind of like a tough woman who's on a first name-basis with auto parts."

She smiled weakly. "I can't go out with you, Mr. Powell. Not on a date."

"Bryce. And you're annihilating my vanity, dear. But that aside, Ryan's not going to take it kindly if you make him renege, and neither am I." Marlie still looked as if she had an itch she couldn't scratch. He supposed he knew why. "I didn't show much finesse when I propositioned you the other night, Marlie. Under normal circumstances I hardly ever ask a woman to bed with me before I ask her to dinner. In your case, proper order is even more imperative, considering your nephew's attitude toward male competition." He smiled. "I shudder to think what might happen if we got caught sharing the same sheets."

Getting caught didn't worry Marlie nearly as much as being in the position to get caught. Bryce Powell was attractive, no point in denying it. Kissing him had been more than pleasant, though she refused to give him a rating. Rex had also been good-looking and an adequate kisser, though in the end, both had amounted to a diddle in their relationship. No more being led astray by tactile attributes, right, Stynhearst?

"I shudder to think about that, too, Mr. Powell," she agreed stoutly. "Maybe we should settle for something a bit more restrained."

"Like what?" he asked, indulging her with a pretense of interest as he turned her around to face him.

Marlie's gaze slid from his face to his chest. "How about friendship?"

"Is that less dangerous?"

She closed her eyes briefly, allowing a unchallenged wave of disappointment to wash over her, then said flatly, "Yes, Mr. Powell. Friendship offers far less peril to both our well-being."

"*Bryce*," he enunciated. "If you call me Mr. Powell again, I might have to breathe some fire. As to your observation on peril, obviously I can't disagree. But male fantasies die hard, Marlie. When I envision myself chatting in the backyard with my pretty chum, there's something missing from the picture."

"It's the fence," she proposed curtly. "You threatened to build one, and you're doing a fine job of it."

Bryce picked up a brunette curl laying enticingly on her breast. The silky strands wrapped around his finger, clinging to him as he wished the rest of her would feel inclined to do. "No more fences. Go out with me."

Marlie fretted, boxed in by her hard-won wisdom. Soon, very soon, she would be turning over her most precious possession into this man's care. Intimate involvement with Ryan's father would be suicide to a sensible, long-term relation. "Couldn't we *try* being just friends, Bryce?" she asked, using his given name to highlight her willingness to trend in a friendly direction.

"Oh, we could try anything, Marlie. The question is whether I would live through it. If I'm to sacrifice myself for a woman, I'd like to know I went with at least a smile on my face.''

Marlie swallowed a reluctant laugh. Bryce had a valid fear. She knew she wouldn't tangle with Ryan in a protective mood. But Ryan couldn't keep her safe forever. It wasn't a question of wanting, but needing, to meet this man on some kind of common ground. With the deck reshuffled, she had to rethink her strategy, for a date hadn't been part of it.

Okay, she thought, resigned. No big deal. "To save Ryan's reputation, I'll go with you to a park for a little sightseeing tomorrow afternoon."

"Sorry, Sunny," he said. "I'm a working stiff. I haven't had a Saturday off since my great depression." Holding on to her arms so she couldn't get away, he added, "I'll pick you up at four o'clock, and we'll do a little sightseeing, eat, then . . . we'll see. Okay?"

"I suppose it's pointless to mention that I have a little boy and no baby-sitter," she said in a voice of mostly decayed patience.

"I'll get the sitter. Mrs. Cobb owes me a huge favor," Bryce said sardonically, digging in his heels when Marlie would shove him out the door. He wasn't to be rushed. He tugged her into his embrace, wrangled a lip alignment and kissed her. When he finished exploring the possibilities of her limited participation, he let her go, grinning knowingly. "I'll see you tomorrow at four," he said, and left.

Alone, Marlie slumped against the wall and stared at the toes of her black patent pumps. Sometimes it was a disadvantage knowing oneself so well. Marlie did, so it made her accountable for her behavior. A woman raised without a loving family tended to seek affection where available, and Marlie was no exception. In defense of her virtue, she had devised a moderated code of frigidity, a frigidity born of caution, not indifference.

Through the years, the male half of Marlie's sophisticated acquaintances had shown her a thing or two about the art of kissing, even kissing of the French influence, with a focus on greater intimacy. And through those same years,

Marlie had shown those same male companions a thing or two about the art of saying no, and meaning it.

With Bryce, she wanted to show off her binational expertise. With Bryce, she wanted to say yes. She had fought it; with all her assumed frigidity, she had fought it. She had kept her lips firmly sealed against another sophisticated invasion, and triumphed—barely.

But what about the next time?

Of all men, why did Bryce Powell have the power to corrupt her carefully controlled libido?

No answers were written on the toes of her pumps. Dispirited, she gathered up strength and finally made it up the stairs to Ryan's door. She pressed an ear to the panel, heard the mysterious rhyme being softly chanted and entered the room to find Ryan crouched in the corner. She joined him there and asked the standard question, "What's wrong?"

Ryan shrugged and offered her his standard answer, "Nothing." But the tears welling in his eyes made a fibber out of him. Needing her reassurance much more than he feared her anger, he looked up at her and asked, "You aren't real mad at me for losing you in that game, are you, Aunt Marlie?"

Marlie sighed heavily. "Well, I can't say that I'm exactly overjoyed at being gambled away. What made you do such a thing?"

"I thought I could beat him. Then he'd stay away from you. But I lost, and now I have to let him have you."

"He can't have me, Ryan," she said firmly. "I'll go on one date with him, which is all your fault. But that's all."

"Do you promise, Aunt Marlie? You won't ever leave me, will you?" He pressed her cheeks within his small hands and tugged her desperately closer. "You have to teach me to throw a ball and all the other things real boys do. I can't start first grade without knowing that stuff."

Marlie wrapped her arms around his squirming body and rocked him like the child he was. Genius carried its own burden that only another of like intellect could truly understand. Most children were taught to be students; Ryan was a student wanting to be a child. He so anxiously wanted to be like other children, but he often didn't understand them, nor they him.

How well Marlie understood his fear of rejection. Learning the games that children play had been the compromise he had accepted in order to become one of them. Teaching him the games had been the challenge she had accepted on his behalf.

"I'll not let you down, sport," she promised softly. "We're a team, remember? We need each other."

Ryan nodded against her chest, and with his assurance renewed, he climbed into bed. Marlie turned out the light and smoothed his blond curls as he drifted off to sleep, while silent tears slipped down her cheeks. She didn't believe that anyone, not even a father, could love Ryan more than she. But her love for Ryan didn't count. Her need for Ryan didn't count. And least of all, her want of Ryan didn't count. What counted was that Ryan belonged to someone else, a man Marlie couldn't even say she liked. But that didn't count either.

Saturday dawned with a gloomy temperament, but grudgingly gave way to modest sunshine by four o'clock. Marlie and Ryan, both dressed in jeans and T-shirts, were waiting at the Saab when a grim-faced Bryce joined them, similarly attired.

"You're obviously a slave to your emotions, Bryce Powell," Marlie commented, determined to put a happy face on this error in judgment. "One moment you're acting almost human, complete with smile. The next, well . . ."

"I'm always human, Marlie Stynhearst, as you will soon find out. The only thing I'm a slave to is other people's wholehearted endeavor to screw up my plans." He motioned to Ryan. "We'll have a short chaperon until Mrs. Cobb returns from another one of her mercy missions."

Bryce was the only one vexed with this unexpected reprieve. Ryan piled into the back seat of the Saab while Marlie leapt lightly into the front. Bryce followed more sedately, frowning. "Don't get too high on relief, dear," he growled sotto voce as he leaned in her direction to wiggle the car keys from his pocket. "Mrs. Cobb will be back in a couple of hours, then the rest of the night will be ours alone.''

Marlie smiled her most insincere smile. "Don't threaten me, Bryce," she whispered back. "I didn't lose at Battling Baboons, and I'm here to humor a little boy, not a big one.''

Bryce's returned smile *was* boyish, his dimples dotting the exclamation of amusement in his blue eyes. "We'll venture into the difference between little boys and big boys when your loaded pistol isn't aimed at the back of my head,'' he said, motioning toward Ryan.

Marlie had decided not to allow Bryce to buy her dinner, for she remembered what he'd said could come after a meal the last time they had discussed the proper order of these things. That was why the delicious roast beef sandwich and home-fried potatoes Bryce insisted on feeding her kept backwashing through her digestive system.

Over lemon meringue pie, Bryce brought her up to date on an old farmhouse he was having remodeled and the need to make a quick trip out to it to check on the progress.

"I'd like to see your new house," she said promptly, hoping that seeing where Ryan would be living would make it easier for her to let him go.

Bryce looked surprised, but not displeased with her eagerness. He paid the bill, giving her a dirty look when she insisted she would pay for hers and Ryan's meals. "Call me old-fashioned, but when I ask a woman out, I expect to pay for it, Marlie," he growled.

"But—"

He croaked a finger to beckon her, and when she met him halfway over the table, he whispered in her ear, "Hush.''

Marlie hushed and left for the car in a huff. Turning Ryan over to Bryce for the remainder of the child's formative years was a sobering thought. Just what the female half of the population needed: a father-and-son duo of harmonized male chauvinism.

Her mood lightened during the short drive to Bryce's house as the pastoral beauty of the landscape whizzed by her open window. Rolling fields and meadows lay in patches of green and brown, seamed together with endless lines of age-old rock fences. Ryan commentated on the trip, comparing the roadside trees and wildflowers with pictures he'd seen in books, and very likely, in his own mind given his extraordinary memory retention.

Within minutes from town, Bryce was turning onto a long, gently ascending gravel drive. When they reached the top, the surrounding countryside stretched before them. Sunnydale lay in the valley below them, scattered amid the green foliage like colorful veggies in a salad bowl. In wonder, Marlie stared at Bryce's restored farmhouse. It could have sprouted from the rich earth, so perfect was its setting. "Your home is beautiful, Bryce," she said simply.

Bryce looked at the traditional two-story, painted white with forest-green shutters, seeing what Marlie saw, but differently. He and Janette had purchased this house and land six months before their son's birth, with kids and dogs and wide open spaces for romping in mind. After Gordon's disappearance, Janette lost interest in remodeling the house; they never lived in it.

Bryce still thought often of Janette and Gordon and the dreams that might have been, though mourning them had finally ended. He could appreciate the fond memories of the past, then release them, like a pristine snowfall yields its beauty to the warmth of a promising sun.

This house had stood waiting for two years, silently offering Bryce a chance to bring him contentment. A few months ago, he decided to grant himself that chance.

Standing on the wraparound porch, Bryce pointed west over the tops of towering elms, poplars and beeches, and told Marlie, "Hartford's about twenty miles from here. AirShip Freight has a landing strip, hangars, office and warehouse at a private airport east of Hartford."

"AirShip? Is that where you put in your time as a working stiff?"

He grinned. "Yeah. It's been an interesting challenge to resurrect a doomed company, but it seems to be happening slowly but surely. You are talking to the lock, stock, and barrel owner of Powell's AirShip Freighting Company, dear. The rewards and the headaches are mine, all mine."

Financial assistance could be a way for Marlie to insinuate herself within the Powell domain. Carefully, she negotiated the tricky waters ahead. "Was it poor economy that effected your business adversely?"

For a moment Bryce watched Ryan and a neighbor's golden retriever romp happily on the green terraced lawn as he wondered how to answer her question. There were no secrets in this little town; everyone knew most of the circumstances of Bryce Powell hitting the skids two years ago. Anyone Marlie cared to ask could tell her all about it—if they hadn't already. Why not be honest?

Taking advantage of their privacy, Bryce led Marlie to a bench swing at the end of the porch. "No, Marlie, it wasn't poor economy, it was self-pity that nearly finished off AirShip," he confessed, picking up her hand and lacing his fingers with hers. "You're very politely tiptoeing around the rumors that I'm sure you've heard. I'll give it to you firsthand, so you won't have to wonder."

He nudged the swing into gentle motion and began relating as much as he could bear of the most miserable time in his life. When he finished, he turned to her. "I lost it, Marlie. I couldn't handle it, so I made friends with a bottle and tried drinking myself into oblivion. Then I made friends with someone who had something better to offer, and things have been improving ever since."

Marlie's chest heaved with the effort of drawing breath through a constricted windpipe. She should ask him questions; it was the natural thing to do since he'd opened the conversation. But she didn't want to know the details of his life with Janette, or the details of Ryan, which she probably knew better than Bryce did. Rather, she should be the one sharing Ryan's past with his father, the years that should have been his, but had been mercifully diverted to her. Bryce's loss had been her gain, and she at least owed him a tour by imagination through the precious years he'd missed.

You should tell him now, she thought wretchedly. Tell him that all wasn't lost, that he has a son, and things can improve even more. But she couldn't push those words out. Instead, she muttered the generically appropriate words of a sympathetic stranger and left her conscience unappeased.

Bryce smiled at Marlie, feeling a strange comfort from baring his soul to her. He abandoned the swing, pulling

Marlie up with him. "Come on," he said briskly. "Let's look at the house. I didn't bring you out here to cry on your shoulder."

Marlie nodded, but offered no comment as she followed him inside. The front door opened into a large, airy living room. A huge stone fireplace extended the length of one wall, a long oak staircase another. A few boxes sat on the hardwood floor of the otherwise barren room. Bryce glanced at the boxes, then quickly away. "They're filled with memorabilia," he said woodenly. "They'll go in the attic when I have time."

Bryce showed her through all ten rooms of the house, each one bare of any adornment. "I'm not much of a hand at decorating. Right now I'm not worried about the niceties, just privacy and some peace," he explained.

Again she offered no comment. Time was pressing upon her, and she knew she must open the conversation of his missing son. Tonight? Tomorrow? Would waiting a few more days be so wrong? She followed Bryce back downstairs, vacillating between telling him now, later or possibly never, which kept creeping in as she silently rehearsed her confession.

In the end, the decision was not hers to make.

Ryan, with his typical curiosity, had entered the house and was presently sneaking a peek into those boxes on the living room floor. In his exploration, he'd discovered a small silver horn. Marlie and Bryce had reached the bottom of the staircase just as Ryan began to chant.

"Born of faith, love and joy,
My child, don't be forlorn.
Play for us your song of hope,
Upon this silver horn."

Marlie thought nothing of the child relating the rhyme to the little instrument in hand, until she looked at the expression on Bryce's face. The man looked as if he'd been turned to stone.

# Four

---

"**D**ear Lord," Marlie whispered. For now she knew where Ryan had learned the rhyme. Before she could do anything, Bryce lunged at Ryan, grasping his arms, shaking him.

"Where did you hear that rhyme?" he shouted at the child.

Ryan looked at Marlie, too frightened and bewildered to answer. She rushed to Bryce's side and pulled against the vise of his hands. "Bryce," she murmured frantically, "you're terrifying the child. Please, let him go. I can tell you what you want to know."

Slowly her words penetrated his conscience, and Bryce released the boy. He straightened and looked at her, a maelstrom of emotions in his eyes. Finally a shudder ripped through his body, releasing him from a terrible spell cast by the resurged past.

The child had wrapped his arms around Marlie's waist and turned his face away from Bryce. "I'm sorry," Bryce muttered, still slightly disoriented by his loss of control. He had frightened the child, and unintentional though it was, he felt badly. He knelt on one knee beside the boy and patted his trembling shoulders. "I didn't mean to scare you, Ryan. Did I hurt you?"

Ryan cautiously turned to Bryce, his face still white. "N-No," he stammered.

Marlie pulled Ryan away from her and gave him a hard-earned smile. "Why don't you go outside and wait for me on the porch swing? Mr. Powell and I need to talk."

Ryan quickly consented, not that she believed for a second he wouldn't. She wanted to run, too, for the moment of truth had arrived. Before she could begin to tell Bryce the news she had been saving for weeks, he was speaking.

"I didn't mean to lose control like that," he said, running forked fingers through his hair in agitation. "When I heard Ryan recite that poem, I went nuts." He shoved his hands into his pockets, walked over to a window and stared out. "I need to talk to him, Marlie," he said more calmly than he felt. "That little horn he found belonged to my son. The poem he was reciting was taught to Gordon by his mother. If Ryan can remember where he heard the poem, there may again be hope of finding my child."

Marlie cleared her throat. Fear twisted her fingers together into painful knots. Her words came out like deeply rooted wisdom teeth. "You've already found him, Bryce."

She thought she'd prepared herself for any reaction from Bryce, but she hadn't. He stiffened, as if her words were vicious blades driven into his back. He slowly turned to her, his face wiped clean of expression. "What did you say?" he asked.

"Ryan is your son, Bryce. I've brought him back to you."

Bryce seemed to explode at her from across the room, one moment a rock of impenetrable stillness, the next, a rush of intensely heated ire. His hands gripped her arms until her bones ached. His face pressed near hers, a mask of ugly accusations and disbelief. "You're lying," he snarled.

Fear writhed in the pit of her stomach. Yet, with vivid clarity, she understood and sympathized with his contradicting emotions. Bryce was afraid to believe. She touched his face with gentle fingertips, instilling a sense of reality to her words. "He's alive, Bryce. Ryan is your son."

He let her go then, and she watched as he assessed her words, applying logic and order to chaotic perceptions. Mere seconds measured the degrees of his returning composure.

"I think you have a lot to tell me, Marlie Stynhearst," he said, almost serenely. "We'll start with the easy stuff. Who are you?"

Marlie began to relax. The worst was over; she could reason with him now. "I'm Marlena Stynhearst. Ryan started calling me Marlie when he first came to me."

A muscle twitched along Bryce's jaw. "You and Ryan have been living in Los Angeles all these years?"

"For three years. He's been with me since my brother and his wife were killed in a accident. Bryce—"

"Did you know how your brother and his wife went about getting this child?"

"No. Not at first, but—"

"I'll admit that the boy with you does have a striking resemblance to Gordon," he said casually. "The age fits, and certainly reciting the poem adds authenticity. How much do you want for the kid?"

Marlie drew in a sharp breath. "How much?" she asked, unable to find any logic in the question. "Ryan isn't for sale, Bryce. I brought him back because—"

Bryce slashed a hand through the air impatiently. "Let's cut the crap, honey. My son's been missing for almost five years, and you're expecting me to believe that he's turned up on my doorstep, fit as a fiddle?"

He shook his head, vexed at being taken for a fool. He'd been warned to expect this kind of thing—a crackpot showing up with his lost child in tow. Bryce had thought that was over with several years ago. He shook his head angrily. It just goes to prove that some people would try anything.

Yet Marlie Stynhearst knew something about Gordon. Or the boy did. The rhyme he recited had been known only by Gordon, it being written for him by his mother. Wary excitement scraped over Bryce's nerves like a currycomb. Could his son be alive? Could he trust this woman or the boy to tell him the truth? That he may not be able to disappointed him as much as angered him. There had been such wondrous promise in meeting Marlie. Now that promise could be a vicious trap awaiting him.

Unwilling to show his mixed feelings, he asked her nonchalantly, "What do you want with the reward money? Did you and your Rex discover that three's a crowd."

Marlie shook with anger until she felt her bones clank together. The monster. The unfeeling, idiotic monster. She'd been through hell and back to get Ryan safely home. Now he thought she wanted money for Ryan's return? With more nerve than she thought she possessed she walked over to Bryce. Facing him squarely, arms akimbo, she set him straight on the financial end of this matter.

"What would I want with your money? Your dear little AirShip facilities could cover the town of Sunnydale from one city limit to the other, plus employ every man and woman in residence, and it *still* wouldn't fill a hip pocket of Stynhearst Industries." She tapped her chest. "And I am Stynhearst Industries."

Bryce studied her a moment, judging her words, judging her. Finally he shrugged, an eyebrow hiked. "Time will tell, won't it? For now, I'll give your noble intentions the benefit of the doubt. So why did you bring my long-lost child home to me? Did it just come to you one day that maybe you should return the child to his father?"

"If you'll stop being a sarcastic, bullheaded brute, I'll be happy to tell you the whole story," she snapped.

Bryce grabbed her arm in an ungentle vice, pulled her over to the staircase and pushed her down on the bottom step. Bracing a foot beside her hip, he crossed his forearms over his knee and leaned close to her face. "I'll be as sarcastic and bullheaded as I please until I get answers to my questions. My son was kidnapped. That child with you knows something about him. So, talk. Tell me your entire, fascinating story."

Marlie licked her dry lips. Reminiscences of another time and place when she was trapped and cowed by a man curled viciously through her mind. She would become a victim again if she allowed it.

She lifted her chin and straightened her spine. She'd done nothing wrong; she wasn't the villain. "You heard Ryan recite the poem. If it were taught to your son by his mother, who else could Ryan be?''

"Any child can learn a poem," he said impatiently. "My first thought was that your kid had heard it from mine."

Marlie nodded. "Farfetched, but possible," she agreed. "If you'll hand me my purse from beside the front door, I'll show you more proof."

He complied, tossing her shoulder bag into her lap. From the zippered compartment, she pulled a small, leather-bound photo album. It contained a visual chronicle of Ryan's years, photos of a toddler, which Marlie had salvaged from her brother's personal effects, and photos she had added over the years.

She handed the album to Bryce. "Your proof," she said simply.

If someone had asked Bryce how he felt at this moment, he doubted seriously that he could have given a sensible answer. Too much nebulous hope was tied up in the moment, and he had experienced it all before—the high of daring to believe that a lead would give him back his son, only to discover that it was nothing more than a puff of smoke in a stiff breeze.

Admittedly, Bryce had never felt this close to the truth. It was a living presence in the room, beckoning him to believe one more time. With hands that would not stop trembling, he opened the book.

The first photograph was of a grinning child who Bryce had last seen nearly five years ago. Gordon. Bryce had spent happy hours enticing that same dimpled smile from those chubby cheeks, and the impish blue eyes could belong to no other.

The next photo depicted the same child, though his features had aged slightly. Bryce turned away from Marlie and braced his back against the newel post. Marlie's gentle hand upon his shoulder and her words, "I'll wait outside," barely registered. The world could have come to an end and still nothing would have distracted Bryce as he looked at picture after picture that charted the natural progression of months and years of a little boy whom Bryce remembered best as a baby swinging joyfully on the patio.

By the time Bryce closed the little album, his cheeks were wet. He breathed deeply, evenly, forcing himself to think one thought at a time, to feel one sensation at a time. It wasn't easy; too much wanted to come at him too quickly. Gordon was alive. Gordon was home. He was waiting outside, waiting with the woman who had known his son for more years than he had. Bryce wanted to rage and rejoice at the same time, for so much had been lost, yet so much waited to be reclaimed.

He wiped a hand across his face and slid the album into his hip pocket. The most uncertain steps he had ever taken in his life consisted of walking out the front door and facing a woman and a child. What did he say to his son who he hadn't seen, hadn't touched, in four and a half years? And what did he say to the woman who'd had the pleasure he'd been denied?

Looking at the two standing together on his porch, Bryce saw nothing but a solid force of resistance against him. The child wore a wary expression that should never have been cast upon a father, and Marlie wore a similar expression of wariness, though she took greater care in trying to hide it.

Oh, but Marlie Stynhearst was wary. She knew things. She knew things that Bryce wanted, needed, to know. But until he severed the solid bond between his son and this woman, he couldn't get his answers.

"I want to show you something," he said to the little boy, and took him by the hand to lead him away from the woman who had already had him for too long.

"Bryce," she called, and he could detect several emotions in her voice—all worthy their presence.

"Stay there," he called back to her. "I'll be back in a few minutes."

Marlie watched from the porch as Bryce led Ryan into a thick grove of birch and oak behind the house. Wringing her hands, she worried about what Bryce would tell the child. Had she done the wrong thing in not telling Ryan that they were traveling to Connecticut to meet his father?

At the time, it hadn't seemed necessary to worry the little boy with a relationship that he understood in principle but not in application. Marlie had been sure that once she, Ryan and the Powells had come to know one another, and the secrets of the past could be revealed, then the future could resume its natural course. A family would be reunited, and Marlie would be welcomed to help connect the past with the present, to help ease Ryan into his new role of son. With a few ill-chosen words, Bryce could make havoc of the delicate situation, and the blame would be Marlie's for not preparing Ryan better.

Bryce returned within the promised few minutes, but he returned alone. "Where's Ryan?" she demanded, searching the wooded edge of the lot. Ryan needed protecting; she couldn't leave him vulnerable for one moment.

Bryce didn't break stride as he mounted the step, grabbed her arm and began hauling her around to the other side of the porch. She dug in her heels, grasped the nearby railing and screamed, "Where's Ryan?"

Her genuine distress moved Bryce enough that he stopped and looked at her. "He's down by the lake, happily playing in an old tree house. Don't worry. He's a lot safer than you are right now, lady."

"You don't understand," she pleaded, refusing to heed his command to follow him. "Ryan—"

Bryce whipped her around, and within barely restrained violence, shoved her against the wall of the house. "You are so right," he snarled in her face. "I don't understand. But I will, or else I'll haul you down to the police station and let you explain it to Officer Vaughn. What will it be, Ms. Stynhearst?"

Ms. Stynhearst? she repeated numbly to herself. Had they regressed to starchy formalities again. The hope within her began dissipating like a morning dew under the hot summer sun as she searched the face of this man whom she had truly wanted to like. He had become a stranger again, as fearful and perhaps more dangerous in his own way than Rex. Had she made no worthwhile impression upon Ryan's father? Was the significance of her being at this place, surrendering her world into his care meaningless to him?

Of course she knew how Bryce felt. She was feeling it too. It was a whiff of fear with each breath she drew, a second of time gone with each beat of her heart. To know that she was going to lose something precious to her could be no easier to accept than waking to find that a thief in the night had visited.

"Please," she whispered to him, "stop hurting me."

The pressure on her arms slackened immediately, and Marlie realized that Bryce thought he was causing her physical pain. How she wished that physical pain was all that needed tending. She rubbed her numb arms and in a voice rusty from contained tears, said, "I know you have questions. I want to answer them for you."

And so she began to talk. She told him everything she knew for certain, and some things that she could only guess. She told him briefly of her life in Europe, of her return to the States to accept her inheritance of the Stynhearst conglomerate, and of taking custody of her small nephew.

The difficult part was confessing her acquaintance with Rex Kane. It embarrassed and shamed her to admit she had been engaged to the man who had committed this horrendous crime against Bryce and Ryan. The same feelings applied to telling Bryce of Rex's threats and blackmail, and of her gullibility in being lead by his evilness.

When her story ended, she looked at Bryce for the first time since she'd begun talking. When he finally asked coldly, "Can you prove any of this?" Marlie thought she might go out of her mind. Scrubbing her hands over her face in agitation, she thought of the cassette tape she'd taken from Rex's safe. It would prove her story. Oh, how she'd personally wanted to bring about Rex's downfall.

Sighing, she knew that Bryce deserved to know that this criminal could be caught and brought to justice. She owed Bryce that much peace of mind, didn't she? "We need a cassette player," she said, pulling the tape from her purse.

Bryce took the tape and motioned her to the Saab. He inserted it into the tape deck, then listened intently as the man, Rex Kane, talked away the next twenty or so years of his life. When the tape ended, Bryce sat still, savoring the first moments of absolute contentment he had experienced in a long time.

Eventually Marlie spoke, breaking the fragile web of peace. "Well?" she asked hesitantly.

Bryce inhaled deeply. Well, indeed. He looked at the beautiful woman beside him and felt regret mixed with hope. "If Nick Vaughn substantiates your story, we'll go from there." He didn't say that investigating would take time, nor what he would do about Marlie while they waited. He wouldn't allow worries about her to distract him now. He had to think of Gordon.

No, not Gordon, he corrected himself savagely. The baby Bryce had known was gone. He'd been replaced by a little stranger named Ryan. Obviously, Bryce was a stranger to the child, too. "Why didn't you tell my son about me?" he demanded angrily.

Marlie's fingers sank into the Saab's plush upholstery. "How, Bryce?" she cried. "How could I tell a six-year-old child about a father he can't remember? He has vague recollections of his adoptive father, but of you, as far as I know, none. I've been Ryan's parental authority for half his life. How could I tell him that I was going to dump him in the lap of a man he didn't know? A man I didn't even know."

Tears drizzled down her cheeks unnoticed as she pleaded with Bryce to understand something that she, herself, could only perceive with her heart. "He's always trusted me to do what was best for him, to take care of him. Abandoning him with a stranger would destroy that trust, and I was not willing to do that. I wanted time for all of us to know one another, to establish a rapport before all the frightening secrets were revealed. Do yourself a favor, Bryce. Don't rush Ryan into a relationship that he doesn't understand, and may, consequently, refuse to accept."

Marlie's unwanted wisdom rang warning bells inside Bryce's head. Hating it because he was denied the thrill of what should be a blessed reunion, he would still take her advice, for he had no wish to jeopardize the future. "Come with me to get my son," he said levelly. "I doubt he'll leave with me without you."

"Where are we going?" she asked.

Bryce didn't answer. Marlie followed, unable to offer herself one good reason for doing so. Bryce was communicating awful predictions in a body language that bode ill for anyone with the nerve to resist.

Crossing a rock fence, Marlie and Bryce waded through the green pasture dotted with bobbing Queen Anne's lace and black-eyed Susans. The short trip ended at a small lake edged with cattails and weeping willows swaying gracefully in the summer breeze. High in the boughs of a nearby elm perched a well-preserved tree house, and through its window beamed the face of a contented child. While Bryce called his son down to go meet a friend, Marlie looked around and saw a good place for a little boy to grow up.

For Marlie, the six-minute drive back to downtown Sunnydale passed with the pleasantness of a small animal caught in a steel trap. The sensation swelled to excruciating proportions when Bryce pulled the Saab into the parking lot of Sunnydale Police Station.

Bryce's friend, Nickolas Vaughn, was a policeman whose physical attributes rivaled Bryce's. After a brief introduction from Bryce and the obligatory offer of assistance from Officer Vaughn, Bryce got right down to the business of destroying Marlie's hope for peace in the foreseeable future.

Since this couldn't be happening to her, Marlie became two women—one standing before the desk of a man in uniform, the other standing back, and with wry humor, listening and watching the proceedings.

She was fingerprinted, then photographed, front and side views. That Bryce and Ryan participated, too, didn't fool her; this degradation was strictly for Marlie's benefit. She was suspect. And Bryce wasn't finished with her yet. He asked Officer Vaughn if he would show her and Ryan the inside of a jail cell. With a quizzical smile, the officer obliged, calling an old man from a back room to lead his "prisoners" to a cell.

Marlie finished wiping away the ink on her fingers with a damp towel provided, she supposed, for fastidious inmates. "May I have my purse now, please?" she requested. Then caustically she added, "I don't carry my hacksaw in it."

The brusque "no" she received from Bryce didn't surprise her. She took Ryan's hand and followed the old man, her head held high despite the cramp in her pride. The metal door of the cell slammed behind her with a finality that was frightening.

While Ryan gave an excited little leap onto the hard, narrow cot of the cell, enjoying this unparalleled entertainment, thoughts ran helter-skelter inside Marlie's head, all tagged with one overpowering theme: Everything was wrong. Impromptu events had derailed logical order, and she was being punished.

Bryce watched Nick Vaughn's eyes following Marlie's departure. He knew what Nick was seeing and felt jealousy explode in his chest like the unexpected detonation of a Molotov cocktail. The untimely, inappropriate sensation was ruthlessly heaved aside as he stepped into his friend's line of vision and stiff-armed his weight against the desk.

Nick's smile managed to convey both innocence and lust. "That sure was fun, Bryce. Mind telling me what we just did?"

Bryce pulled the small photo album from his pocket and handed it to Nick. Nick obligingly opened the cover to the first photograph. "This was your son, Gordon, wasn't it?" he asked quietly.

"Is. That is Gordon. Keep turning the pages."

Nick looked up sharply, then back to the album. He flipped forward, then backward, comparing. The last photo was of the little boy whose fingerprint profile rested on the green desk blotter. Nick didn't have to explain that he had managed to put two and two together to get four. He said, "If artistry is involved, the photographer was damn good." He tapped the photo album against his palm. "I can send these to the lab in D.C. and see what they can tell us."

Bryce straightened, took the album from Nick and returned it to his pocket. "I already know what they'll tell us. The little boy in your jail cell is my son."

Perceptively, Nick raised an skeptical eyebrow. "But...?"

"But he doesn't know it." Bryce sighed and shoved his hands into his pockets. There was nothing that Bryce felt he couldn't tell this man who had shared the worst times of his

life. Nick had made up the entire Sunnydale constabulary at
the time of Gordon's disappearance and had worked harder
than three men to help locate the child. From his time with
the NYPD, Nick was privy to an impressive network of information, and although it hadn't been enough to find
Gordon, Bryce never doubted that the best help had been
available. Why Nick Vaughn had taken his talents and skills
from the big city and brought them to Sunnydale was a
mystery, but no one in this small town was of a mind to
complain.

Bryce played the tape of Rex Kane's confession, then
concluded the tale with why Bryce's elation at being reunited with his son was curtailed by the little boy's attachment to Marlie Stynhearst.

Nick tugged on his bottom lip as he stared thoughtfully
at Bryce for several moments. Finally he said, "You believe
this woman could have had something to do with your son's
actual kidnapping."

"That's what I was hoping you could tell me."

"I can prove or disprove she's Marlie Stynhearst in a few
hours. Proving her guilt or innocent of a four-and-a-half-
year-old kidnapping could take longer." He glanced down
beside his desk. "In the meantime, a lady's handbag can tell
many a secret."

"Be my guest."

Nick grinned. "Not hardly. I'd need a search warrant.
You, on the other hand, are merely a citizen with a wayward nature." He plopped the purse on his desk. "So you
can have the honors, and I'll be your witness that you
swiped none of the contents."

"Thanks," Bryce said dryly. Feeling a bit as though he
were peeking into a lady's lingerie drawer, he dumped the
contents of Marlie's purse onto the desk blotter. He soon got
over his feelings of invading her privacy when a plump roll
of greenbacks followed the usual lipstick, compact and
wallet. Bryce slipped the rubber band off the roll and rifled
the crisp one-hundred-dollar bills. There was way more
money in the wad than a woman could claim to need on
even the most arduous shopping spree.

Nick cleared his throat. "Well, the lady doesn't seem to favor a wallet for conventional purposes. Maybe you should see what she does keep in there."

The lady kept several credit cards, a few bills of reasonable denominations and an ID card. The photo on the card was definitely Marlie—or Marlena, to be exact—Stynhearst of Los Angeles, California, date of birth placing her at age twenty-three.

"Could be fake," Nick said with reluctant practicality. "How about a driver's license?"

"No."

The leather swivel chair sighed against Nick's restless shifting position. "She drove Hap Hanson's truck...illegally it would seem. Anything else of interest in there?"

Bryce was about to say no when a photograph slipped from a slot in the wallet and fell to the desk. He picked it up and examined the man standing beside the woman claiming to be Marlena Stynhearst.

Bryce instantly put the man's face to the name he'd heard recently. "This is Rex Kane," he said, handing the photo to Nick. "About five years ago he approached me with a business proposition that didn't interest me. I thought at the time that with AirShip thriving, I didn't need to make any questionable East Coast transport deals. Kane didn't take my refusal too well."

"No, I guess not, since he decided to kidnap your son a few months later." Nick looked at Bryce steadily. "We're talking about an extremely unstable, potentially dangerous man, Bryce."

Bryce nodded, having already figured out that part. "Can you keep the woman for me a couple of hours while I talk to my son?"

"I can keep her a lot longer than that. Even if the purported Ms. Stynhearst is exactly who she says she is, she's still guilty of withholding evidence in a felony."

Bryce stared at the tape in Nick's hand as if it had suddenly grown horns and a tail. That tape would put his son's kidnapper away for years, but it could also put away Marlie Stynhearst. For more reasons than he cared to admit, he was reluctant to see that happen. He met Nick's eyes as he said softly, "I don't recall telling you where I came across that tape, Nick, and for the life of me, I can't seem to remember."

"Are you sure?"

He looked again at the tape, then back at Nick. "Until I understand what part this woman Stynhearst plays in my son's life, I need her closer at hand than the nearest federal penitentiary."

Nick nodded, but added, "Why don't you accidently forget Ms. Stynhearst's purse? Without her money and credit cards, she'll find her anchor dropped in Sunnydale. I can secure the perimeter of our fair city against other means of escape."

"Sounds sensible," Bryce agreed, inwardly shuddering at Nick's implacable methodicalness. If Marlie was guilty, Nick Vaughn was the man to bring her down hard. "How about springing my son from the slammer?"

Nick scooped the keys up from his desk. "Be careful, Bryce," he advised.

Ryan went with Mr. Powell, not because he wanted to but because Aunt Marlie said he had to. He promised to behave and not play any mean tricks on Mr. Powell, though Ryan had thought of some good ones, and thought Aunt Marlie a spoilsport for denying him.

Ryan and Mr. Powell went to the airfield of AirShip Freighting Company, and the man strapped Ryan into a plane he said was a Piper Cherokee 6. For fun, Mr. Powell placed a radio headset on Ryan's head and while waiting for runway clearance, explained about some of the buttons, knobs and levers used to guide the plane.

It was exciting, for Ryan had never been inside a cockpit during flight. Yet it was confusing because he *wanted* to be in the cockpit with Mr. Powell. For while Mr. Powell did look at Aunt Marlie in a gross, mushy way, he also played a tough game of Battling Baboons. Getting photographed, fingerprinted and sitting in a jail cell at the police station had been cool, too. All that was great, but the rest was awful.

Ryan would never admit it, but, on the inside where it didn't show, Mr. Powell scared him. Scared him more than nightmares, or being without Aunt Marlie or starting first grade without any friends.

Could a person like someone and not like them at the same time? Ryan wondered. He didn't know, but he sure did hate being all mixed up. And it was all Mr. Powell's fault.

Bryce was thinking his own similar adult version of the eccentricities of the human nature. His heart pounded and his palms sweated upon the yoke. He'd taken off from runways hundreds of times in his life, but today was different. Today he carried precious cargo—his son.

How many times had Bryce dreamed, in vain he had thought, of his son being exactly where he was at this moment? Yet, visions of Marlie Stynhearst's fear-ravaged face as she waved goodbye to them from that jail cell chipped away at his contentment. It wasn't right or fair that she intrude upon this moment. Nevertheless, she may as well be sitting beside him, counseling him on the best way to handle this delicate and new situation in which he found himself.

Giving up on ridding his mind of Marlie's haunting presence, he conceded to trying things her way first. His son was home, but many things could affect how he adjusted. With his heart in his throat, Bryce began lightly feeling his way toward that coveted linking of their past, present and future.

"I'm glad you decided to come flying with me," he told the little boy beside him via the headset radio.

"Me, too," Ryan agreed warily, yet truthfully. "I wish Aunt Marlie could have come, too, though."

Bryce's hands flexed upon yoke. "There's only two seats in this plane, son. We'd have had to haul her around in the back like cargo."

Ryan giggled. "She wouldn't have liked that."

Bryce grinned back wryly. "No. Probably not. Besides, we men have to have time to do special things by ourselves once in a while, don't you think?"

The child straightened a bit in his seat and grinned. "Yeah. Do you take lots of men riding in your plane?"

"Not many your age," he said, swallowing hard. "But if I had a son, I'd take him flying with me all the time."

Curiously, Ryan asked, "Why don't you get a son, then?"

Bryce glued his eyes to the windshield of his plane, knowing if he looked at the child beside him, he'd lose it. "I had a son once. A bad man stole him away from me a few years ago."

"Did you love your son a lot?"

"Yes. A lot."

"You could get another son, you know," Ryan said sagaciously. "There's lots of kids who need dads."

Easy, Powell, he warned himself. His heart beat a cadence that threatened to crack his ribs. "What about you? You don't have a dad."

Ryan appeared truly surprised by the question. "I don't need a dad. I have Aunt Marlie."

"There's lots of things your Aunt Marlie can't do that a dad can."

Pursing his lips, Ryan thought this out for several moments. Finally he said, "Maybe. But there's lots of things Aunt Marlie can do that a dad can't, and I love her most in the whole world. So I'm satisfied."

Bryce wanted to raise his fists and bellow in rage at this unfairness. Of course he wouldn't. He'd continue to reason with a six-year-old child who didn't know or care what he was giving away. "Suppose you found a man who wanted to be your dad very much, and who would love you the most in the whole world?"

Ryan grew cautious again. "Who?"

"Me."

For Bryce, the silence in the cockpit was a rubber band being slowly stretched to its limit. Ryan looked at him, genetic replicas of his own blue eyes reaching out to him with sweet, innocent compassion.

"I'm sorry about your little boy getting stolen," Ryan said. "Maybe if I didn't have Aunt Marlie, I could be your son. But Aunt Marlie needs me, Mr. Powell." Sensing that he'd distressed the man, Ryan hurried to add, "But I know how you could still be a dad. Last year in my kindergarten class, there was a boy who wasn't treated very well by his foster parents. I bet he would like to be your son."

Bryce Powell looked at the small boy beside him and manfully presented him with the proverbial stiff upper lip. Where it came from, Bryce had no idea. He had wept bitterly for his lost baby. At the graveside of his wife, his tears had flowed unashamedly. Today's defeat was no less wretched, yet for the sake of this child, he would save his pain for later.

Later, many things would happen. One of them would be calling Marlie Stynhearst to a reckoning. Whether she'd had anything to do with his son's actual kidnapping was almost irrelevant now, for she had taken his child away from him in a far more irrevocable way.

"You lied, Marlie Stynhearst," he whispered darkly. "You did steal my son."

# Five

———

To say Bryce returned to the police station in a damaging frame of mind was like saying that a mad bull turned loose in the small barn could have serious ramifications. He and Ryan retrieved his Aunt Marlie, then Bryce went about his mission with an iron control reminiscent of his earlier years.

They returned to his house in the country, and Bryce sent Marlie inside and shooed Ryan back to the tree house. Knowing how those green eyes of Marlie's could chip away at his resolve, Bryce refused to look at her when he joined her in the living room. With easy mental acrobatics, he could imagine her as only what he wanted her to be—a pretty woman to woo into his arms. But she wasn't. She was deeply enmeshed in the worst nightmare of his life, and he wouldn't allow himself to forget that soon.

He began to pace, trying to put some order to his chaotic thoughts. He wanted to put his hands around Marlie's throat and squeeze the life out her for what he'd been through. Yet, if even one fourth of what she'd told him was the truth, then he couldn't blame her for what had happened years ago. Finally he looked at her patiently watching him from where she sat on the bottom step of the staircase. As he expected, nothing but blasted innocence staring back at him.

"How did your time with Ryan go?" she asked gently.

"I wasn't too encouraged," he responded, keeping his distance by leaning against the stone fireplace across the room.

"He didn't try to bomb your car, did he?" she inquired facetiously, hoping humor would break the unbearable tension.

"No. But he probably would have if you'd suggested it."

"I wouldn't have done that, Bryce," she insisted mildly, wrapping her fidgeting hands around her knees to still them.

Bryce lunged away from the fireplace to stride across the room. Stopping near her, he grasped the newel post in lieu of her more tender body parts. "Wouldn't you?" he ground out. "Why not? You've not spared me much so far."

Marlie's gaze wondered away from Bryce's angry face and focused on the stained-glass transom above the front door. "I never had any desire to hurt you, Bryce. If I had, I wouldn't have given you back your son."

"No!" he bellowed, slashing a hand through the air to emphasize the denial. "You're giving me back a child, yes, but you still have my son, Marlie. You have his love, his loyalty and his respect. How do I get that back?"

Marlie's disadvantage, of course, was that she hadn't thought to examine herself in a criminal light. "I don't understand your attitude, Bryce," she said honestly. "I didn't steal Ryan from you. I simply loved a little boy who needed me, and took for myself what he was willing to give. Why are you blaming me for something that wasn't my fault?"

"You mean, assuming I believe that you had nothing to do with my son's kidnapping?" he retorted, and ignored her sigh of annoyance. "Your question then becomes a matter of objective reasoning, Marlie. Intellectually, I know you'd be right. I couldn't blame you. But I'm not thinking objectively right now. I'm thinking as a father who's been denied his son for almost five years, and who's looking at a woman who's had the pleasure that should have been his."

Turning away from her, he shoved his hands through his hair angrily. "Every time I think of you holding my child on your lap while I was tormenting myself with his fate, I could shake the daylights out of you. For years I've had to wonder if he was alive or dead. Hungry. Abused. I felt every pain I imagined him feeling. I felt the terror and confusion that he must have felt. I bled my life away in tears while you sat in your supposed comfy mansion rocking my child to sleep each night.''

When Marlie stood to cling to the banister, her movement caught his attention. He strode over to her and grasped her arms. "You want to know what it's been like for me?" he demanded, giving her small, jerky shakes to emphasize his inner torment. ''I could show you. I could throw you out of here and keep you away from Ryan for the next five years. Of course you'd still have advantages that I didn't have. You'd know that Ryan was alive and well treated. You'd at least have the hope of seeing him again.''

Marlie was crying, not because of Bryce's rough handling, but because the painful picture he had just painted would eventually become her reality. Couldn't he see this? She swallowed her sobs and searched his furious face. ''I admit that unfortunately your choices in what happens now are few, but not nonexistent. You do have the choice of looking for the blessing of the past. Your son wasn't abused or left hungry. He lived to come back to you. You—''

''And I'm supposed to thank you for your tender mercies in caring for my son,'' Bryce cut in brusquely. ''I was innocent, lady, yet sentenced to five years in a hellish prison of doubts and fears. Then you come along with your Pollyanna good cheer and expect me to thank you, the warden, for setting me free.''

Marlie felt her patience slipping. What did he want from her? ''You can't have it two ways, Bryce,'' she asserted. ''Either you find comfort in knowing that all those fears for your son were groundless, or you wish that he was dead, to justify keeping the heartaches of the past alive.'' She shrugged. ''There's nothing else I can do but reassure you.''

It was the wrong thing to say. Marlie knew it the moment the impulsive words rushed from her mouth. Bryce's eyes flared with an unholy fire that demanded the sacrifice of her very soul for penitence. She shivered slightly as a lazy smile drifted across his face. His voice dripped over her like warm, sweet honey straight out of hell's kitchen.

"Oh, I'm sure I can think of something else you can do, Ms. Stynhearst."

"What?" she asked apprehensively.

"I'll let you know."

"And in the meantime?"

"We wait, Ms. Stynhearst."

Bryce took it into his head to do his waiting on the sofa in Marlie's apartment and nothing short of gunpoint would dissuade him from the notion. Marlie didn't own a gun, which under the circumstances was probably a good thing, so she put a confused and wary Ryan to bed and went to bed herself, leaving the man sitting in her living room. She was so exasperated with him that she didn't offer him even the most modest comforts of her home.

The deliberate oversight bothered her, and as she drifted off to sleep, she acknowledged the reason: Bryce Powell sleeping on her sofa offered her a feeling of safety that she hadn't experienced since fleeing from Rex. That alone deserved a pillow and blanket.

Marlie dressed the following morning in bright yellow shorts and a polka-dot top, their cheerful color meant to bolster her optimism. She hadn't left the entire job to her wardrobe choice, however. While she had showered, she'd devised a plan that could solve many problems. She found Bryce sitting at her kitchen table, his hands wrapped around a steaming mug of coffee. He'd apparently gone back to his apartment to shower and to change his sleep-rumpled clothing for neatly pressed khaki pants and navy polo shirt. She hoped his fresh appearance was indicative of his disposition, for now was the perfect opportunity to discuss her ideas.

She smiled a good morning and reached for another mug. "I've been thinking, Bryce. Now that you know Ryan is your son, I should go back to L.A. and take care of Rex Kane. The man belongs behind bars for what he's done, and the sooner he's there, the sooner we can all rest easier. While

I'm there, I thought I would have my program expansion team start putting together a report on the feasibility of opening a branch of Stynhearst Industries here in Sunnydale and contracting the transport of our products to AirShip. Not only would I be nearby if you and Ryan need me, but I could help insure Ryan's future by investing in your company.''

"Hush, Marlie."

Marlie hushed. The deceptive calmness of the order implied that it was a good idea. She waited, and finally he deigned to explain why he was refusing her offer.

"First of all, you're not to get anywhere near Rex Kane. He's being taken care of, and all you have to do is what you're told. Don't ask again to go back to L.A. Second, I don't want your money or your investments. All I want is my son back, completely mine and happy about the situation. I spent a sleepless night on your short, lumpy couch, deciding the best way you can help me accomplish that.''

"I'm all ears, Mr. Powell," she said frostily, squeezing her coffee mug to keep her hands from shaking.

Bryce got up from the table. To burn nervous energy, he began opening cabinet doors as he continued talking, pretending to look for something for breakfast, and not really noticing there was nothing to be had. "You see, Ms. Stynhearst, it has occurred to me that if I boot you out of Sunnydale, you'd take the heart of my son with you. That could set back our relationship for years, and I've already lost too many of those with him. It appears that if I want my son back, his Aunt Marlie will have to be part of the deal.''

Somehow the relief she should have felt with Bryce's admission that he needed her wasn't there. "I intended to stay until I knew Ryan would be all right with you."

"Did you? That's very commendable.'' He rushed on, knowing if he stopped to dwell on what he was about to do he'd lose his nerve. "Am I to understand that it's within your commendable nature to do anything to help me regain my son?''

"Of course."

Bryce's smile satanically. "Good. You're going to marry me.''

Some invisible imp tried to knock Marlie's legs from beneath her. She grabbed the countertop and hung on. "Your sense of humor leaves a lot to be desired, Mr. Powell," she gasped incredulously.

The smile that bothered Marlie vanished in a blink of the eye. Bryce stalked over to stand before her and smiled another smile that offered no improvement over its predecessor. "I left my sense of humor a few thousand feet above the ground about eighteen hours ago, dear. I've been dead serious ever since."

"But...but...I can't marry you," she wailed.

"Why? Are you already married to Rex Kane?"

"No!"

"Then you can marry me. And you will, in three days."

"You're crazy," she breathed. "You can't make me marry you."

Bryce pursed his lips and tipped his head in agreement. "True. I can't make you say 'I do,' but I can make you wish you had."

Marlie stared at him, her mouth agape. He sounded as if he were taking his insanity seriously. Marlie was tempted to go back to bed so she could wake up from this nightmare. "You haven't been listening, Bryce. I'm not going anywhere until I'm certain Ryan will be all right. I have an apartment, plenty of money and time on my hands. I'll be right here in Sunnydale for as long as it takes to see Ryan happy. Marriage isn't necessary."

"You haven't been listening either, Marlie. You see, dear," he explained with infuriating calmness, "by marrying you, I'm insuring your cooperation. Marriage will also reassure my son that, as his stepmother, you'll be staying around."

Marlie returned to the pragmatic chore of pouring the coffee, needing to salvage something normal in the moment. Yesterday she'd submitted to the indignity of being treated like a common criminal. She'd hated it, but she'd submitted because she understood Bryce's fears. Today she was almost thankful for yesterday's indignities. "For Pete's sake, Bryce," she said, laughing nervously as she tried to fill her mug without spilling the coffee, "yesterday you had me down at the police station being fingerprinted. How can you even suggest marriage, feeling about me the way you do?''

A long, heavy moment passed before Bryce answered, ''It's because of the way I feel about you that I am serious about this marriage, dear. If my son could wave you a cheerful goodbye, it wouldn't be necessary. But he can't, so you'll stay until he can.'' He pinned her to the wall with a look that dared her to doubt him. ''There's very few things I wouldn't be willing to do in order to get my son back.''

He took the coffeepot from her listless hands and placed it on the counter. ''I can tell from the shell-shocked look on your face that you think I'm being ridiculous. But ridiculous or not, you're just going to have to humor me.''

Glancing down past her bright yellow shorts, he frowned at her long, tanned legs, then turned her around and gave her a little shove toward the door. ''Go get ready.''

There was more to get ready for? Marlie wondered hysterically. She hadn't been ready for this much. She dug in her heels, and over her shoulder asked, ''What am I supposed to be getting ready for now? An air raid?''

Bryce almost smiled. ''To sign marriage applications and get blood tests. Now, do you want to go upstairs and dress, or do you want me to carry you up there and dress you myself?'' Seeing the unwilling compliance on Marlie's face, Bryce shook his head sadly. ''That's a pity, Ms. Stynhearst. I never had the pleasure of dressing a woman.''

''But you're quite proficient at moving a woman's clothes the other way, Mr. Powell?''

''I'll let you answer that question yourself in three days,'' he said wryly. ''Unless you're wanting the schedule moved up, I'd suggest you move out. In the meantime, I'll have Mrs. Cobb pick up Ryan. He'll be safe there, and with Nick's kids to play with, he'll be happy with her until after the honeymoon.''

''Officer Vaughn has children?'' she asked, surprised.

Bryce nodded. ''Six-year-old twins—a boy and a girl.''

Her eyebrow raised. ''Funny, but from the way he acted at the police station, I didn't get the idea he was even married.''

''He's not. But his marital status needn't concern you.''

"You're right. It's my own marital status that concerns me, Mr. Powell. I happen to like it the way it is." Before he could raise another debate, she marched out of the kitchen.

Bryce was mistaken about Marlie's obligation to humor him, for she had to do no such thing. Human compassion obligated her to grant patience to a man who had already suffered enough, but there had to be a sensible limit to what she owed him. Marriage was above and beyond all reasonable expectations. This had to occur to him once her identity was verified.

But looking at Bryce now and seeing nothing but raw determination compelled Marlie to grant him—for a while—the humor he seemed to be lacking.

Two hours later, Marlie was reconsidering her generosity. If Bryce had left his humor a few thousand feet in the air yesterday, today hers was hitting rock bottom in the wake of his madness. She signed marriage applications. She surrendered her left arm to the questionable mercies of Betty the Witchnurse at the local clinic. On the fifth painful jab, the woman finally hit Marlie's vein. Her only consolation to the ordeal was that Bryce looked slightly green around the gills and a little regretful that she'd suffered.

He brought her back to her apartment after Katy, the waitress at the only café in Sunnydale, served them a quick lunch. Marlie wanted nothing more than to escape Bryce for a few peaceful moments, but she failed to eject herself from the Saab quickly enough. He grabbed her sore arm, and she gasped before she could check her reaction.

Bryce winced and let her go. "I'm sorry," he said.

"For once we agree on something," she snapped caustically.

His lips tightened. "Don't try to leave town, Marlie," he warned her.

Marlie's chin came up. "You'll find me a woman of my word, Bryce. I said I was staying until Ryan was safe. Now that I see how unstable you are, I have to wonder just who is Ryan's greatest threat. You or Rex Kane." Bryce looked ready to explode, but she refused to relent. "I'll be here until I'm satisfied that Ryan's in good hands."

\* \* \*

Marlie was held prisoner in Sunnydale for the next three days. Bryce was suspiciously absent from the scene, yet everywhere she went in the small town, the power of his influence followed her. She knew she was watched constantly; the Sunnydale citizens were as discreet about their spying as Godzilla hiding behind a lamppost.

She missed Ryan terribly.

Needing to get away from her loneliness and the oppressive feeling of being surrounded by the enemy, Marlie went to Happy Hanson, hoping to rent his truck for a drive in the country. Happy didn't look as happy as usual. He gently but firmly refused the request, saying he had orders not to give his truck to strangers. Unbelievably, Mrs. Cobb entertained the same attitude, refusing to allow her to see Ryan.

It was like being back at boarding school, but worse; Marlie felt more alone than she'd ever been in her life and it frightened her. The whole town had branded her an outcast, and hatred for what Bryce had done burned in her breast. He had turned them all against her, and now, even if she managed to work out some arrangement to stay in Sunnydale, to open a branch of Stynhearst here, there would be a wall built of mistrust existing between herself and the townspeople.

At the end of Marlie's third day in exile, she saw a smiling Nick Vaughn walking toward her. She took no pleasure from the friendly overture; he was a friend of Bryce Powell's, which in this town translated as no friend of hers. She turned around, ignoring the man's call to wait.

A moment later, he was beside her. "Mind if I walk you home, Ms. Stynhearst?" he asked politely, easily matching her quick pace.

"Yes," she answered with equal politeness. It made no impression. Officer Vaughn avoided a hint as if it might give him a rash. His tolerant chuckle scrubbed at her nerves.

"I've come bearing good news, Ms. Stynhearst. Good news that rightfully should be told to Bryce first, but since I happened to see you alone—"

"Alone?" she said feigning incredulity. "Am I alone? My head's been in such a whirl lately, I hadn't noticed."

Nick nodded, passing her a commiserating smile. "I am sorry. But until we found out something about you, we couldn't take the chance of you leaving town. I told Mr. McFarland at the bus station not to sell you any tickets. From there, the news traveled via the town grapevine that you were suspected of something, though the townspeople didn't know what." He looked at her keenly. "Sunnydale protects its own, Ms. Stynhearst."

"And very thoroughly, too, Officer Vaughn. I've lived in some of the meanest cities in the world, but the Sunnydale inhabitants make street people look like Spanky and Our Gang."

"I think we can safely say that's behind you now. I got the confirmation on your identity and credentials a couple of hours ago."

"Well, that's a relief. I've been wondering if I was who I thought I was." Her eyes cut across to him. "I am, aren't I?"

Nick laughed. "You are. And it's truly a pleasure to meet you Ms. Marlena Stynhearst of Los Angeles, California, owner of Stynhearst Industries."

The brisk walk became a stroll. Marlie wasn't one to hold a grudge when someone was at least trying to be reasonable. And Nick Vaughn was. "I could have saved you a lot of trouble if you'd believed me in the first place," she said softly.

"Call me Nick, please. And I did."

Marlie looked at him sharply. "You did?"

"Uh-huh. Before I came to Sunnydale, I was a police detective in one of those cities you mentioned," he said. "So many shifty-eyed characters come through the precincts every day that a cop gets so he can hear a lie before a suspect even opens his mouth." He looked at Marlie and smiled. "Your mouth never struck me as suspicious, Ms. Stynhearst, though I couldn't take a chance of guessing wrong."

Marlie smiled back and felt better than she had in days. She had the law on her side now, and soon the Sunnydale residents would follow. Of course that accounted for less than half the opposition, since Bryce, alone, made up the majority of her troubles.

Nick took the house keys from Marlie's hand, unlocked the door and ushered her into the foyer. "I just wanted to stop by and tell you that Bryce should be a little easier to get along with from now on."

"That would be nice, but what would thrill me more is for Bryce to call off his insane wedding plans," she said pointedly.

Nick looked sincerely puzzled. "What wedding plans?"

"The ones I've been humoring him with," she said sardonically.

Nick took his time before answering. "Most men take their brides-to-be for a blood test, Marlie, not to be fingerprinted."

Marlie nodded agreement. "He's done that, too," she said, pulling up the three-quarter sleeve of her jersey shirt to display a large, ugly bruise on the inside of her elbow. "I've received the full Bryce Powell treatment. Naturally, now that he'll know who I am, he'll call a halt to this craziness, right?"

Nick Vaughn looked so doubtful that Marlie wanted to cry. "I won't marry him, Nick," she grated, physically trembling as she thought of the possibility.

"Hey, Marlie, don't worry until you have a reason," Nick gently chided, sliding a comforting arm around her.

As inopportune times go, this one ranked near disastrous. Bryce came through Marlie's front door, found his best friend and his fiancée in a cozy clinch and saw red. "What are you doing?" he asked of either who had the nerve to answer him.

Nick did. He held on to Marlie and replied flippantly, "I'm stealing this beautiful woman from under your nose."

"Friendship has its limits, Nick," Bryce said coolly.

Nick cocked an eyebrow, and a slow, understanding smile dawned. "So it does," he responded, stepping away from Marlie.

Marlie looked from one man to the other, catching the gist of their exchange and not liking it. She pointed an admonishing finger at Nick's nose. "You tell Bryce your news this instant," she ordered, employing a tone she usually reserved for a mischievous Ryan.

Nick chuckled and complied. "Her ID and story check out, Bryce. You can lighten up on her now."

Bryce ignored the wisecrack. "I'll talk to you tomorrow, Officer Vaughn," he mumbled. Then, with a hand between the man's shoulder blades, he energetically helped Nick over the threshold and slammed the door after him.

The atmosphere in the foyer was thick with animosity and too tough for the fragile silence. Marlie faced Bryce squarely. "Now that you know I'm not a Jezebel out to do you dirty, can we begin to make some sensible plans for the future?"

Bryce narrowed his eyes. "I see nothing wrong with the plans I've already made."

"But... but Nick just told you—"

"I know what Nick just told me." He interrupted her. "But that you're who and what you claim doesn't affect my problem."

"Marrying me won't, either," she argued. She shook her head, marveling at this intelligent man's obtuseness. "I understand and sympathize with your doubts and fears, Bryce, but I won't create a new problem when I already know that it can't alleviate an old one. I'm sorry, but I can't accept your marriage proposal."

"Ms. Stynhearst, you don't know how sorry you can be. I wasn't proposing anything, I was telling you that you will marry me."

Marlie grappled for control of her life as one fights for the last breath on the third time down. "And if I refuse?" she asked in a hoarse whisper.

"If you refuse, Ms. Stynhearst, you'll force me to employ some very unpleasant legal action. For instance, I could turn you over to Nick for withholding vital evidence of a felony. Or I could obtain a court order that would deny you any rights to ever see Ryan again."

Stunned, Marlie stared at Bryce Powell. A black pall of inevitability closed around her as she acknowledged his power over her.

It had happened again. Marlie had simply fled from one blackmailer straight into the hands of another.

There had to be another way. Somehow two people should be able to transcend the hurts of the past and the fears of the future and concentrate on their one common denominator: a little boy who needed love and security.

Unlike Bryce who was operating on pure emotions, Marlie would not allow him to dictate a perfectly awful solution when better ones were in the offering. Desperately she began to bargain.

"There are other ways to approach this problem, Bryce. I can live with you and Ryan. Your house is large. I could have a room..." Marlie's very logical solution petered out as Bryce shook his head.

She gritted her teeth. The man was being deliberately obstinate, with a bit of hatefulness thrown in for good measure. "Just what's the problem with sharing living space?" she demanded. "People do it all the time, and with less good reason."

Oh, but Bryce was tempted to take Marlie up on her offer. If Ryan wasn't around to consider, Bryce would move Marlie into his house so fast she wouldn't remember packing. But Ryan had to be considered. What two consenting adults did with their private lives was one thing, but asking an impressionable child to participate was another. It smacked so hard of irresponsibility that Bryce physically felt the sting. He couldn't even fuss at Marlie for suggesting such a thing, for he could tell she was simply working through a list of pragmatic alternatives. He'd spent the past two nights doing the same thing himself, only to discover that there weren't any.

"Marlie, you seem to be missing the point of this marriage," he asserted. "I have no intention of living with a woman while my son occupies the same house. Kids see marriage as a permanent commitment. I want him to know that I will keep both you and him around, and hopefully he will begin to see me in the father role of a family unit, not merely as a boyfriend of here today, gone tomorrow status. I won't disillusion him with offering less."

"Disillusion him?" she demanded. "Bryce, you're not thinking straight. Nothing will disillusion Ryan more quickly than what you're doing. He won't understand or accept a sham of a marriage. He's too perceptive for that. He never liked Rex. He hated the idea of our marriage, and did everything he could to discourage it. And do I have to remind you of the reception you received?"

Bryce shrugged. "That's your problem, honey. You'd better think of a way to convince my son that I'm the best thing to come along since sliced bread. If you fail, you lose as well as I."

Threats. Always a man's last resort. Well, this time she'd call a bluff. "I will not marry you," she said simply. "So I guess you'll have to cart me off to jail."

With Marlie following, Bryce walked into the living room, picked up the phone on the end table and punched some numbers. He held her gaze steadily as he spoke into the receiver. "Hello, Nick. Bryce. I just remembered where I came across that cassette tape of Kane's confession. You won't believe it, but—"

"Please, don't."

He placed a hand over the receiver. "Pardon me?" he asked politely.

"I said, please don't," Marlie repeated through gritted teeth.

He nodded. "Sorry, Nick. Another memory lapse," he said, and hung up the phone before Marlie could hear the lady on the other end relating the local time and temperature.

Marlie looked ready to spit nails; Bryce couldn't much blame her. He wasn't proud of his deception; on the contrary, he felt lower than a snake's belly button.

What could he give her to make up for what he was taking away? His bitter memories were of a time not so long ago when his life had crumbled in his hands. The emotional ruins were unfit to offer a woman like Marlie. She didn't need his modest wealth. And his home was boxed up in the apartment two doors down, waiting to be moved to an unfurnished house. His bleak inventory produced one conclusion: only his body was worth sharing.

He wondered what old Art Newton would say about what Bryce was doing, then dismissed the thought as one of those things he'd rather not know. There was no other choice. He would take Marlena Stynhearst, and she would belong to him until...

Here, a blank future scrolled through his mind. How long would Marlie belong to him? He didn't know, but she was his for now.

Marlie saw Bryce reaching for her and flinched away from him. Oh, he had it all planned, didn't he? He'd said taking her was part of the deal. She'd see that he didn't.

His hands persisted, eluding her restraint and tenderly cupping her face. He stirred the hair at her temples with gentle breath, its fine current drifting over her eyelids and downward to her lips. Kneading fingers worked the tense cords of her neck and shoulders. Smooth, cool lips warmed themselves against the heated rush of her sporadic breathing. He worked on her senses, chipping away at her resistance until Eve's serpent uncoiled within Marlie. Her arms and mouth disobeyed her and reached for the forbidden fruit. Just one nibble, she promised herself as she inhaled the scents of Bryce's maleness.

The taste of him was sweet. It lingered, tempting her to enhance its flavor by partaking of the fullest measure. She inched closer to him, her breasts finding a perfect place against his ribs. She practiced her woman's skills, using her tongue to duel with the devil's, turning his own temptation back upon him.

Their hands worked in unison, discarding clothes and finding mutual delight in the difference in their contours. His palms tested the weight of her soft breasts. Her fingertips searched for the strength in the plains of his chest. And the sweet bonding of their lips could last forever.

Marlie waltzed on air, unwittingly celebrating the downfall of her resolve, until the great serpent within her smiled, baring fangs that pricked her awareness. Reality came in small spurts. The scratchy sofa fabric against her bare back. The cool air upon her damp skin. A rasping zipper in the quiet room. What *was* she doing? She hated this man. Didn't she?

Not giving a foolish answer a chance, she wedged her arms between their chests and gave a mighty shove. With a grunt and a few choice words, Bryce landed on the floor.

"What's the matter with you?" he demanded, getting to his feet.

Marlie snatched her shirt from the floor and with quick but shaky fingers pulled it over her nakedness. She stood up and smiled at him with chilly courtesy. "Nothing. I'm just fine now."

Bryce pitched his weight to one hip and braced his fist upon it, clearly exasperated with her thoughtlessness. "We'll be married tomorrow, Marlie," he reminded her pointedly. "What difference does it make if we share a bed one night early?"

Marlie looked at the pillows and blanket innocently reposed at the end of the sofa where Bryce had spent the past three nights. *I've already shared your bed, with near disastrous results,* she ruminated moodily. To him, she coldly replied, "But we aren't married yet. And—" she picked up the pillows and blanket and slammed them into his chest "—we don't want to disillusion your son, do we?"

"Marlie!" he said sharply, halting her in retreat.

She spun around. "I will not marry you, Bryce Powell," she snapped. "I'll think of some way to convince you of that fact."

"Come hell or high water, Marlie, you're marrying me tomorrow. Resign yourself to that fact."

*"I will not marry you, Bryce Powell."*

# Six

Marlie married Bryce Powell the following evening.

As it turned out, Bryce was a man of his word. Hell came sweeping in on the shirttail of a storm that raised every stream and river in eastern Connecticut. Despite the deluge, Bryce Truman Powell took Marlena Theodora Stynhearst as his lawful, if unwilling, bride.

In the sanctuary of the Sunnydale Congregational Church, Marlie stood before Art Newton, a kindly old preacher who'd been shipped in from Hartford to sanctify the vile deed, and softly repeated the traditional vows that she had no intention of ever keeping. She vindicated her contrariness with simple reasoning: if the marriage failed to be consummated, the vows would be negated.

In fairness, Marlie had tried to warn Bryce of her nonconformity to tradition in this case. But her warning had fallen by the wayside, much like all the other times she had attempted to reason with the man. For Bryce, the shortest distance between Marlie's defiance and his own way was the use of one four-letter word—*hush*.

Marlie suspected that Bryce's mama had started telling him at birth that he showed potential for despotism, for one had to start young to learn how to put so much authority in one little word. Marlie had hushed, all right, but had also felt shamefully smug with the gleeful anticipation of slamming her bedroom door shut in the autocrat's face tonight. She owed the man no other favor than giving her best attempt at warning him that his conjugal rights where destined to wistful thinking.

Marlie halted on the church steps. "Okay, Mr. Powell, it's time we had another little talk."

Bryce kept walking. "Hush, Marlie. It's done, and I'm tired of arguing."

A disgruntled frown slashed across her face. She couldn't imagine why he was tired of arguing since she'd been doing all the talking, leaving him with the easy jobs of saying "hush" and looking tough and grim. Marlie had the unsettling feeling that if she didn't exert herself a bit more, she would be pressed ever more tightly into a corner with no exit. Being an expert on corners, she decided to take a leaf from the book of her two expert tutors and practice a little assertiveness herself. "Don't turn your back on me as if I don't exist, Bryce Powell," she told him quietly.

Bryce turned slowly, his mouth tipped up slightly with amusement. He shrugged, then casually leaned against the fluted column of the church entrance, arms and ankles crossed, mutely telling her that he could humor a woman who'd unfortunately lost all her marbles. "You had something else to say?" he inquired, needling her with a condescending chuckle.

Ignoring it, she nodded. "For the record, I'm not staying with you because I fear your threats. I'm staying to be near Ryan. With that in mind, I want to know what happens now that we're married."

He shrugged again. "Nothing so different from your original plan, I imagine. Think of our marriage as getting what you want, but it coming with a hefty price tag. You wanted to invest in my son's future. A ring on your finger shouldn't cost you too much."

"And when you're satisfied that you've won Ryan's affections, will you grant me visitation rights?" she persisted.

Bryce stared at her a long moment. He knew he wasn't being entirely fair. A blind man could see how much the woman loved Ryan; the evidence of her handiwork was obvious in the healthy, happy little boy she had returned to him. Stripping Marlie of all hope was too cruel, yet making rash promises didn't serve his purpose. He compromised. "We'll see."

You're darn right we'll see, Marlie wanted to shout at his retreating back. She hadn't sneaked away from a maniac, dragged Ryan across a continent and agreed to a farce of a marriage, just to end up losing what she wanted most.

The ride home from the church was accomplished in silence, yet the clamor inside the heads of the recently wedded couple could have raised the dead.

Bryce was thinking about the reasons why Marlie had actually consented to marrying him. Sure, he could see to it that charges were brought against her for withholding evidence in a kidnapping. He could deny Marlie visitation rights, too. But surely she knew that to follow through with either threat was a spitefulness beneath him.

No, Ms. Stynhearst was a smart lady and had to know she held all the trumps in this game. Married to him, she now legally lived in Bryce's home with Ryan, who despised his father, and Marlie could take her own sweet time about changing the circumstances of either.

When she calmed down and got over her initial indignation of being manipulated, she was bound to realize her advantage. Making love to her, binding her to him physically was his only means of maintaining any control. Was that expecting too much?

Marlie's thoughts ran counter to Bryce's, yet around the same circle. She hadn't calmed down from being manipulated, and she vowed never to recover from her indignation, but neither condition put a damper on her conscience. She knew she could take advantage of this marriage by keeping a wedge between father and son, thus extending her own time with Ryan. She'd considered those possibilities for all of thirty seconds before reluctantly dismissing them as a spitefulness beneath her.

She had come to Sunnydale to reunite Ryan with his father; that hadn't changed. Though she couldn't find much praise for Bryce's draconian tactics for gaining her cooperation, she was trying to remain magnanimous about his insecurities. All bets were off, however, if he pushed for a consummation of vows.

The newlyweds returned to Marlie's apartment, where they were to spend their supposed honeymoon, then set up housekeeping. They parted in the front foyer, Marlie to the bedroom to change from her ivory suit, and Bryce to the kitchen to investigate its tantalizing aromas.

He followed his nose to the oven, where he found a mouth-watering lasagna bubbling. Ah, the work of dear Mrs. Cobb. He'd eaten enough of the lady's meals to know what a treat he and Marlie had in store.

While he busied his hands with setting a romantic table, his mind and body sneaked ahead an hour or two in delightful anticipation of having Marlie serve up his dessert. She had made all the expected noises of a woman submitting to a reluctant marriage, but he didn't believe she meant half her threats. No sex in their marriage? Hah! He'd held her in his arms and felt the tremors of her so-called averse response. She wanted him as much as he wanted her. At least tonight he would be putting to rest one shared torment.

Surveying his and Mrs. Cobb's efforts in the culinary department, he nodded in satisfaction. The stage was set. He sat himself down at the head of the table to wait for his bride to join him.

He waited. And waited.

Finally it became obvious to Bryce that his blushing—with anger—bride had either given him the slip or a cold shoulder. He hoped it was just the latter as he rushed to the bottom of the stairs and bellowed, "Marlie!"

The hairbrush in Marlie's hand clattered into the bathroom sink as she flinched at the ineloquent summons. "Well, it's about time," she muttered peevishly. Frankly, she was surprised that it had taken Bryce this long to figure out that she wasn't coming down to share Mrs. Cobb's little lovers' banquet that she had smelled as soon as Bryce had opened the front door.

Could Bryce be suffering from a bout of patience? Marlie snorted. Stupidity would be as likely an answer to his tardiness as patience, and Marlie didn't believe Bryce was stupid, either. He'd probably lost track of the time as he plotted his next move to ruin her life.

She tightened the sash of her white silk kimono, pinched a little color into her bloodless cheeks, then flung open the bathroom door. Marlie had been doing some plotting of her own the past thirty minutes. Advancing to the top of the stairs, she quickly glanced at the floor to her right to make certain that all she needed for a peaceful night's sleep was where she left it. It was. She stood akimbo, legs braced, shooting her husband a green-eyed glare that just dared him to try taking the stairs that separated them.

Bryce might have taken up that challenge if he had been in any condition to. But Marlie stood with her back to the brightly lit bathroom, and what the light exposed through the thin silk of her robe left little to the imagination. The blood in his brain made a waterfall descent to lower regions, leaving him fancifully light-headed as he stared at the shimmering white-garbed angel above him. Mercy, she was lovely. Marlie possessed a body that defied human flaw.

"I wish you'd either shut your mouth or do something sensible with it," Marlie snapped. His mouth did shut, then twisted into a devilish smile. Of course, with a suggestion like she just gave, why shouldn't it? She might as well have doused the situation with gasoline and dropped a match on it. Then, as he started to act on his heated thoughts, she intercepted his actions. Both arms flung outward, palms forward in self-defense when Bryce raised a foot to the next riser.

"Stop!" she commanded, and was surprised to see that it worked—sort of. He still strained forward like a runner ready to take the next hurdle.

"Perhaps I didn't make my position clear when I agreed to marry you," she said. "To repeat myself, my position will not be anywhere in the vicinity of yours, especially at night."

Bryce slumped against the wall, woefully shaking his head. "Marlie, it isn't I who's confused about positions. *I* know what positions we'll both be in, especially at night. I told you that I wanted Ryan to see this as a real marriage. Did you really think that this was going to be a marriage of convenience?"

"I most certainly did not. There's not one thing convenient about it for me."

"We can do this marriage civilized or we can do it mean, Marlie. The choice is yours," he said, though he didn't mean it. "What's it going to be?"

A pillow and two blankets sailed down the staircase to land at Bryce's feet for an answer. He sighed. So be it.

Bryce took the stairs in three bounds and clasped her in his arms, wedging her into a corner. "Do you recall the old saying, I think the lady doth protest too much?" he whispered as his hands crept up her rib cage.

Marlie tried pushing those two five-tentacled marauders away from their goal. "Do you recall the old saying, you get what you blackmail?" she said through clenched teeth.

"I don't think that's quite the way the old saying goes, dear," he murmured, chuckling. His warm breath entered her ear and streaked a path to her toes, lighting the entire switchboard of erogenous receptors as it traveled. "It is in my experience," she flung back, her voice off-key with breathlessness.

The knot of her sash loosened and his big warm hands slid across her bare midriff. She wasn't nude under her robe, but what covered the essentials was silk and lace and practically invisible to the naked eye.

Marlie squeezed her eyes shut, and against her will, she was propelled backward five weeks and three thousand miles. But a different body was pressing her into a corner, and the sharp blade slicing through her was not made of steel but of manipulating words that drained her of will and independence.

Marlie knew no sensible reason why fear was curiously absent at this moment. The situation was as volatile and dangerous as those moments under Rex's knife. But unlike Rex who had held her life by the strength of his hands, Bryce held her in a bondage that enslaved the spirit. For that freedom she would fight.

Unfortunately, her fearlessness made her careless. One of those shocking, untrue hyperboles slipped out in the heat of the battle. "I'd rather be dead than to go to bed with you," she rasped.

Bryce stiffened, his arms falling to his sides. He turned ghastly white, and for scant moments his body fused with inert energy. Before Marlie could even regret her unworthy pronouncement, he was upon her, his monstrous rage charging the air around them. "Don't ever say you'd rather be dead than alive. Do you hear me?" he snarled through bared teeth.

"I...I—" Marlie's sputtering agreement was cut short when Bryce's weight bore her harder into the sharp edge of the banister. She gasped in mingled fear and discomfort, but her complaint went unheeded. Bryce's next harsh words wiped all thoughts of appeasing him from her mind.

"Janette thought death was preferable to life, too, but had she stuck it out with me, she might have believed differently today."

Marlie's eyes widened as she realized what Bryce's was saying. Surely he hadn't meant it the way it could be taken. "Mrs. Cobb said your...your...wife was killed at a railroad crossing," she stammered, not wanting to know, but needing to know, regardless.

Like a dreamer checking back in with the rest of the world, Bryce blinked a couple of times and focused on Marlie's face. He pushed himself away from her and sank onto a step. "She was," he said wearily, staring down at his clasped hands dangling between his knees. "It just didn't happen the way most people believe."

Raising his head, Bryce stared out at nothing, his voice inflected with emptiness. "Some people thought the brakes failed when Janette came to the railroad crossing. Some thought she must have had the radio on too loud and couldn't hear the train approaching. Others thought that she had been daydreaming again and didn't realize the train was upon her. If I hadn't known better, I would have believed the latter speculation.''

He sighed heavily, allowing his thoughts to carry him deeper into the past. ''If you ever wondered where Ryan got his genius, it was from his mother. Janette was the most intellectually brilliant woman I'd ever met, but when she took off on one of her meditative odysseys, anything could happen.'' He smiled absently. ''Once she came home from the supermarket and realized that she'd left Gordon sitting in a grocery cart at the produce counter. By the time I got there to retrieve him, he had plucked ten dollars' worth of grapes off their stems.''

The smile vanished. ''She also left Gordon in his patio swing while she went into the house for the forgotten barbecue utensils. When she came back out he was gone. Regardless of how many times I tried to tell her it was something I might have done myself, she never could forgive herself for leaving him alone. That's one of the reasons I know she wasn't daydreaming the night she died. Janette didn't daydream much after Gordon was taken. Reality had become too real to let her out of its grip.''

When several moments passed and Bryce remained silent, Marlie prodded him gently, sensing he needed to lighten a burden. ''It could have been brake failure, Bryce,'' she said softly.

''No. It wasn't. Janette started drinking after Gordon was taken. I used to follow her to drive her home, but she'd make awful scenes if I insisted, so I relented, telling myself that she wasn't drunk. That last night she really wasn't. When I went to get her, she calmly told me that she was fine. And I believed her. Hell, I begged myself to believe her. I wanted to believe that maybe one more nightmare was finally coming to an end.''

His hand came up to unconsciously grip the banister. ''I followed her to the railroad crossing and watched her brake lights flash twice before she released them and coasted into the path of that train. Whether she intended the brake lights to be a signal of her intention or just a final farewell to me, I'll never know. But I do know she understood exactly what she was doing.''

Marlie closed her eyes and saw the crisp imagery of horror that Bryce had witnessed as he watched his wife die. His agony became real to her, eclipsing her own nebulous perceptions of losing someone dear. "I'm sorry," she whispered, regretting the inadequacy of the trite condolence.

Bryce twisted around and leaned on his elbow beside her feet. "Are you?" he asked, his voice betraying his barely banked anger. "You don't know half of what you've to be sorry for, Marlie. It took Janette five years to conceive our son, and after a dangerous birth, she could have no more children. While you were holding our only child in your arms, my wife was driving into the path of an oncoming train because she believed him dead."

Bryce rued his words too late. He was blaming the wrong person for Janette's death, and he knew it. Wrapped up in his own world of self-pity, he had missed the signs of Janette's instability. He had killed her with his failures. He had killed her with his weaknesses. He, not Marlie, had pushed Janette in front of that train.

Finding his son offered Bryce a chance at redemption from his past mistakes. Everything had to be perfect to make that happen, and Marlie was a necessary part of the plan. There would be no violence in their bed, but the power of seduction was a fair weapon. He could wait one more night to use it.

He looked up into Marlie's pretty face now ravaged with sorrow. "You can trot off to your solitary bed without fear of me torturing your pride tonight," he said levelly, snatching up the pillow and blankets from the steps. "But tomorrow night will be different, Marlie. My son will be here and I want him to get the idea that the arrangement is happy and permanent. I will sleep with you, we will act in all ways like a husband and wife, and in the end you may find that the arrangement has its compensations."

It was noon when Marlie opened her swollen eyes. She sat up in bed and clutched the block of wood posing as her head. "That's what you get for crying instead of sleeping, idiot," she muttered. But those tears had seemed to help wash away some of the bitterness of her own defeat.

She'd cried for poor Janette who'd paid a horrendous price for her losses. She'd cried for poor Bryce who'd paid for a debt that wasn't his own. She'd cried for little Ryan, the innocent prize for which so much had been wagered and lost. There had been tears of regret for Rex's greedy madness. And finally, there had been tears of anxiety for Marlie's duties of bringing wholeness to a family of which she could never be a part.

Those duties began today and there was no justification in stalling. Marlie headed for a cold, wake-up shower, which helped, but not that much. Neither did the cup of instant coffee and the pain-reliever tablets she had for lunch.

She made her daily call to Stynhearst, speaking to her personal secretary who had to first complain about the ponderous duties thrust upon her by irresponsible management. Then she finally reached the part of her report that interested Marlie. Rex had left Stynhearst on an extended business trip. His destination was unknown, as was the time of his return.

Was he chasing the red herring she left for him in Canada? Hopefully. Regardless of Rex's whereabouts, Marlie was acutely aware of hers and Ryan's vulnerability.

Faced with a choice between moping around an apartment, worrying or taking on dear Mrs. Cobb and the whole darn town of Sunnydale if necessary to get Ryan back home where he belonged, Marlie chose the latter with gusto.

All that bravado was wasted, however.

"Ryan is at a neighboring town playing at my grandsons' home," Mrs. Cobb informed her coolly.

Marlie could have pounded her head against the brick building for her stupidity in allowing Ryan to be taken away from her, then pounded Bryce's head too, for his equal part in this foolishness. Was she the only one taking Rex Kane and his threats seriously?

As if hearing the agony in Marlie's mute question, Mrs. Cobb responded not unkindly, "Little Ryan is in safe hands, Ms. Stynhearst."

Marlie opened her mouth to remind the landlady that the "Ms. Stynhearst" was no longer correct, but Mrs. Cobb allowed no interruption. "I don't know the details of this quarrel between you and Bryce, but I sense that Ryan is in the center of it. Bryce wouldn't allow the child to come to harm just to spite you."

Marlie believed that. Bryce would protect his son. But she would also like to live long enough to see Ryan grow up. Four years in a boarding school had taught Marlie self-reliance. She was a doer, and turning to someone for help was a concept as foreign to her as expecting someone to volunteer. Yet she understood the value of friends; she needed the townspeople on her side. Alone, she was a sitting duck.

Mending the fences that Bryce had torn down for her seemed a reasonable place to start. "It was kind of you to leave dinner for us last night, Mrs. Cobb. I do have you to thank, don't I?"

Mrs. Cobb smiled a little then. "You're welcome. Bryce said you weren't...uh...too handy in the kitchen, and asked if I would leave a meal for you in the oven."

Marlie's own smile was puzzled. "For me? Didn't you intend for Bryce to have any?"

The question seemed to fluster the older woman. "Well, I certainly didn't mind if Bryce shared the lasagna, but... uh... under the circumstances, I wouldn't have expected it."

Under the circumstances? Mrs. Cobb didn't expect Marlie to share a meal with her new husband? A dark suspicion was growing out of this peculiar conversation. "Do you know what Bryce and I did last night, Mrs. Cobb?" she asked inanely, then blushed the identical shade of red as the other woman when she realized how that could be taken. And was.

"Really, Ms. Stynhearst. I don't pry into Bryce's personal...affairs."

Oh! she seethed. He hadn't even told his friends that they had married. Nor, from dear Mrs. Cobb's attitude, had he informed these people that she wasn't the town pariah any longer.

Marlie left Mrs. Cobb and continued working her way through Sunnydale, testing her theory that Bryce hadn't informed anyone of his recent nuptials. By the end of the day, Marlie was convinced, to tears, that she had been correct.

The eyes of the town were certainly upon her, but not kindly. Dear old Hap Hanson wouldn't even look her in the eye as he refused to rent her his truck. Not that his cooperation would have helped much. Marlie really wasn't prepared to press Mrs. Cobb for directions to Ryan's whereabouts. Even her hopeful ally, Nick Vaughn, was unable to lend her support, being called away on police business. Marlie returned home late in the afternoon, alone and lonely.

Since Ryan had come into her life, loneliness had become an improbability. With him gone, the feeling returned, creeping up behind her, enveloping her in the stark awareness of only her own mere presence. Loneliness victimized loneliness, preying upon its insecurities. She pulled the drapes closed against the sight of the unfriendly little town, then dithered around the apartment, working her nerves into something like shredded cabbage.

When the front door lock rattled, every self-protective instinct went on red alert. When the unidentified male intruder ventured into the shadowy living room, Marlie's self-protective instincts did their job, plus some.

She let loose a scream that would make a banshee blanch, bounced the TV remote control off the man's broad chest, then went for the throat. It was a remorseless, automatic attack intended to maim, or worse. The problem was, it was totally ineffective. Bryce Powell was simply too big for her to bring down.

By the time Marlie realized it was Bryce's windpipe under her fingers, the man had easily disengaged himself from combat, pushed her onto the sofa and covered her squirming body with his own considerable bulk. Her hitherto lethal hands were grasped within the iron fists of her victim and trapped beneath her own weight on the sofa.

Bryce lowered his face close to Marlie's. "That's some welcome you've perfected, dear," Bryce said, quite conversationally, too, considering his blue eyes were snapping like two bullwhips. "But a simple kiss and a 'hello, honey, I'm glad you're home' would do just as well."

Bryce's soothing words were all it took to bring Marlie to her senses. Relief left her giddy. A giggle quickly avalanched into nearly hysterical laughter, which produced a steady trickle of tears that pooled in the rims of her ears. Wasn't it funny? At the rate things were going, no husband in history would regret more the occasion of ignoring his wife.

Bryce held his position and patiently waited out Marlie's inappropriate levity. Finally he said calmly, "Marlie, would you mind telling me what I did to deserve a charge from the Light Brigade?"

In Marlie's opinion, pride, like beauty, should be more than skin-deep, if it was to be meaningful. If Bryce didn't care that her life was in jeopardy, she'd take care of the problem herself. "You left the lid off the peanut butter jar," she snapped. "Now get off me, you big lug. You weigh a ton."

Ignoring the insult and the order, Bryce settled his hips deeper into the space between her thighs. "I did not leave the lid off the peanut butter," he responded roundly. He then added meaningfully, "We can't afford to lose one of the three food items you keep in this house."

"No one invited you for breakfast, Powell," she reminded him absently. For her true attention was centered on their centers and how their ridges and hollows fit together with intimate perfection. Given a few more minutes to lose her anger, Marlie might have appreciated, or at least worried about what was happening between them from the navel down. As it was, Bryce had to move quickly to keep her from nipping his lower lip when he tried to kiss her.

"You have a vile temper, lady," he growled.

Her temper? "You're about to twist my arms off and you still have the nerve to criticize my temper?"

The pressure on her arms instantly lessened. "If you don't calm down and start talking sense, the pain in your arms will be the least of your complaints. Now tell me what's wrong."

Marlie sniffed once, twice. Too many of the words that she didn't want said came soggily tumbling out. "Nothing, you insensitive jerk! Nothing but that everybody in this heartless town treats me as if I were Typhoid Mary resurrected on the courthouse lawn."

She squeezed her eyes shut and tried to stem the flow of determined tears, but it didn't work. Somehow during the deluge, everything changed, including her position on the sofa. When she opened her blurry eyes, Bryce's shirt buttons were directly under her runny nose and the steady beat on his heart echoed in her waterlogged ears.

"Details, Marlie," he requested softly, but he figured he already knew them and he felt terrible about it. He and Nick had been so busy talking to the authorities about Rex Kane and making plans for keeping Marlie and Ryan safe that Bryce had forgotten to spread the message that would dispel the notion that Marlie was suspected of some crime.

But Marlie made him pay for his oversight. She gave a little wiggle with her backside that burrowed her more deeply between his thighs. The friction created by the cruel maneuver nearly set his lap on fire.

"You want details?" she demanded, squirming around to face him. He gritted his teeth and nodded, then endured five minutes of ill-tempered explanations augmented with flailing arms and wildly gyrating hips. Thinking that she'd never come to the end of her animated recitation, he grabbed her hands and gasped out, "I get the message. All of it. I'm sorry. I'll take care of it, if only you'll stop making me suffer for my negligence."

"You're suffering?" Marlie demanded. "Just how are you suffering?"

He cocked an eyebrow, then lifted his hips until they made complete contact with the seat of her shorts. Marlie's eyes widened until they resembled the bottoms of two green cola bottles. Her mouth rounded in a silent "oh." Despite her sophisticated upbringing, dealing with male arousal was absent from her repertoire of experiences. But as Bryce had claimed to get her message, she was also getting his message, for no woman living in the twentieth century could fail to know why male body parts changed size.

Marlie leapt from Bryce's lap, embarrassment scorching her cheeks, and stammered out, of all things, an apology.

"Oh, that's okay," he assured her, grinning like a shark. "I intend to let you make it up to me later." Before she could contest his brag, he continued smoothly, "And I'll make up for my little mistake now. I'll make dinner reservations for you, Ryan and me at the country club for tonight. By noon tomorrow, at the latest, the entire county will know that you have my seal of approval.''

''Whoopee,'' she said with a sneer. ''Will you also tell them that you married me, or will you go on letting them believe that I'm shacked up with you?''

Bryce almost laughed aloud, but thought better of it. Marlie was in a true snit, and the plans he had for later tonight called for a placated woman. He settled for giving her a dose of gentle sarcasm. ''For a woman who offered to do just that, you seem hell-bent on claiming the name if not the game now.''

''You just forget about the game, Bryce Powell,'' she ordered. ''As for your name, it has suddenly become useful. You're apparently one of the powers that be in this community. When I open Stynhearst here, I expect the Powell name to pull some weight.''

Ominously, Bryce pulled all that Powell weight up from the sofa and walked over to where Marlie was trying not to melt under the glare of his wrath. ''I told you what I want from you. Money can't buy it.''

Courage, Marlie. Remember that corner. ''But money can buy what I want, Bryce. Even when you think you have Ryan where you want him, part of him will still belong to me. I won't let you kick me out of Sunnydale when this is over. I'm going to plant roots here. I'm going to have a legitimate reason to return time and time again. You can bar me from legal visitation, but you can't stop me from building a physical reminder of the life he once shared with me. He'll always remember, because I won't let him forget.''

''You'd turn this into a nasty custody battle?'' he asked tightly.

She quickly shook her head. ''No. There's no question of who's to have custody. Ryan's your son, and he belongs with you. But I'm his Aunt Marlie, and all I'm asking is for you to respect the title.''

Bryce took a deep breath, aware that the conversation had somehow veered dangerously off course. Too many other plans could go awry if he persisted in beating this topic into the ground. He offered a truce. ''All you're asking is that I learn to share my son.'' He smiled a little. ''Be warned,

Marlie. I never liked to share my new toys on Christmas morning, either.''

Marlie visibly relaxed and smiled back. ''Sharing is a virtue with its own rewards. Share your son with his Aunt Marlie and you'll end up with a happier child.''

He shrugged. ''Maybe.'' When she would have followed up with another lecture on virtue, he lay a finger across her lips and said, ''I'm hungry.'' The callused pad of his finger gently chafed her bottom lip. ''Actually, I'm of two appetites. One for a prime rib at the country club and the other for a chunk of a tough, cantankerous, argumentative, frustrating female.''

Marlie ducked away from his gently abrasive touch, yet the tip of her tongue ventured out to collect the lingering tingle, before she replied. ''Best settle for the prime rib, Bryce. The other is out of season.''

He grinned knowingly. ''We'll check the menu again later tonight. In the meantime, I'll go to my apartment and get cleaned up while you go over to Mrs. Cobb's and collect Ryan.''

Marlie crossed her arms over her chest, and didn't have to work at all to obtain the annoyed look. ''I tried that this afternoon. Mrs. Cobb barred the door with a mean frown and meat cleaver.''

Bryce looked surprised. ''No kidding? She frowned at you?''

She almost smiled. ''I exaggerated. She softly scowled.''

Bryce started for the door. ''No more scowls. I promise,'' he said over his shoulder. Hand on the doorknob, he turned back and added, ''While you're at it, you may as well tell Ryan about our marriage and start edifying him on the joys of obtaining a father.'' Then he was gone.

''The coward,'' Marlie muttered. How was she to explain a marriage, which she didn't understand herself, to a bright, all-together too intuitive child like Ryan?

Marlie went back to Mrs. Cobb's to fetch Ryan, who seemed happy to see his aunt, but reluctant to have left his new friends in the neighboring town. Promises of returning soon got Ryan back to the apartment, where Marlie pulled him between her knees and grasped his slim waist, then went about her dirty job with the finesse of a floundering mud turtle in over its head. Inanely, she began the discussion with an in-depth history of medieval matrimonial customs. By the time she got to the part about bridal dowries and family alliance, Ryan was eight centuries ahead of her.

"Are you going to marry somebody?" the boy asked incredulously.

Marlie cleared her throat—three times. Drat Bryce Powell! "Actually," she said hesitantly. "I already have."

Ryan's face crumpled. "Mr. Powell?" he guessed fatalistically.

"Yes."

"But you don't love him, Aunt Marlie," he wailed.

Marlie wanted to wring her hands. She wanted to wring Bryce's neck. There was a maximum weight limit set on the lies she was willing to tell Ryan. Despite Bryce's notions that this marriage appear normal, declaring love where no love existed would be an awesome mistake.

"No, Ryan, I don't love Mr. Powell, and he doesn't love me. But remember what I just told you about the old days? There's different reasons for getting married. Mr. Powell and I got married for business purposes. You see, I've decided to start a branch of Stynhearst here in Sunnydale, and much of the shipping will be handled by Mr. Powell's freight company. If we're married, all the profit stays in the family. Doesn't that make good economical sense? You can think of this marriage as a family alliance. Okay?"

All that sounded so reasonable, she was tempted to believe it herself. Only Marlie knew better, and from the look on Ryan's suspicious little face, so did he.

"Aunt Marlie, we could leave," he said solemnly. "We don't have to stay here with him."

Oh, Ryan, she groaned silently. If only we could pack up and run away from our troubles. But she had packed up and run away once before and trouble stayed hot on her heels. It was out there. She made no bones about admitting she was frightened of Rex, but the worry was her own, and not to be shared with an innocent little boy. "I made a promise, Ryan," she said gently. "You wouldn't want me to welsh on a promise, would you?"

Ryan didn't look too happy about the turn of events as he shook his head. Marlie wouldn't be a bit surprised if, despite her best efforts, Barf Dater didn't press his cape and shine up his helmet for another go at eliminating the competition. Extracting promises of good behavior would be meaningless unless the little boy chose to accept Bryce. Marlie would do her part to instigate a smooth reunion, but the bulk of work had to be done by Bryce. Marlie hoped Bryce was prepared for a stretch of rocky road.

# Seven

Supper at the country club went atrociously. Marlie was pretty sure that the prime rib didn't really taste like an old army boot, but her rapidly decaying disposition managed to taint everything around her. Bryce saw through his promise to promote for her a better standing in the community. When he threw in the news that he had married the rich little industrialist from L.A., the lewd looks that passed between the men turned speculative. It was insulting. Even more so because Bryce, with all his outrage over taking any of her money, didn't seem to mind that the people thought that a hasty marriage for the sake of lust, now had the added appeal of a sensible, lucrative arrangement.

The disaster over, Marlie took Ryan's hand and stalked back to the car. When Bryce eventually joined her there, she ordered him to take her back to her apartment. She'd had about all the indignities she cared to suffer for one day, and a raging headache had crowned the occasion. Once back home, Marlie jumped from the car and slammed her way into the apartment, unknowing, maybe even uncaring, that Ryan had failed to follow.

Back in the Saab, both males stared at the front door that still quivered on its hinges. Bryce gripped the stirring wheel, grinding his teeth. Ryan leaned over the front seat, his brow puckered into a frown.

"I don't think my Aunt Marlie wanted to marry you, Mr. Powell," Ryan claimed.

Bryce smiled wryly. "What makes you think that?"

"Because she doesn't act like it."

"Oh? Did she act differently when she was engaged to Rex Kane?"

"Yeah. She acted sort of silly. All smiley and giggly."

Bryce had to agree that Marlie wasn't smiley or giggly. "Kane must have done quite a number on her," he commented drily, mostly to himself. But Ryan startled him by agreeing.

"Yeah. It was really yucky. I tried to tell Aunt Marlie that Rex was a creep, but she wouldn't listen. I told her that when she wasn't watching, Rex looked at her with mean eyes and a mean smile. Aunt Marlie said that Rex couldn't help the way he looked, and she didn't believe he was playing her..." He stopped, searching for the word his aunt had used.

Bryce supplied it for him. "False?"

"Yeah. False. But he was. Rex Kane looked mean."

Shaking his head in amazement of his son's intuitiveness, Bryce made a mental note to watch how he looked at people when he was around this child. Many adults would have been taken in by Kane's cunning act. Marlie had been. He wondered how many other things his son had noticed that others had missed.

"Did Rex Kane or anyone else ever mistreat you, Ryan?" he asked gently.

The boy shook his head. "Aunt Marlie wouldn't let that happen. One time Rex told her that she should send me away to a private school for geniuses, but she got so mad at him that he didn't bring it up anymore." He frowned ominously. "Aunt Marlie and I take care of each other."

Bryce twisted around in the seat and raised an a challenging eyebrow. "Is that a warning, young man?"

"Yes, sir. I'll do anything to keep Aunt Marlie from being unhappy."

Bryce nodded, accepting the child's conditions for a peaceful settlement of differences.

Marlie's bedroom door opened and the object of all her misery walked nonchalantly into the room, his arms loaded with blankets and pillows. Marlie's chin came up, for she knew what *that* meant. "I have to go put Ryan to bed," she said haughtily, intending to sweep by him.

Bryce dropped his load and caught her arm, pulling her around to face him. "You're not running away, are you?" he asked, amused.

"No," she said, tugging on her arm, even as she told the white lie. "I happen to be where I belong. You're the one who's displaced."

Hanging on to the only part of Marlie's body he felt safe in handling at the moment, Bryce shook his head in honest confusion. "Why does the thought of going to bed with me seem to send you in such a tailspin? In all modesty, Marlie, I honestly believe I could have coaxed you there without the benefit of wedding ring. Doesn't making an honest woman out of you count for anything?"

"I was an honest woman before I fell into your clutches, Bryce Powell," she snapped. "Associating with you has done nothing for my reputation."

"What's that supposed to mean?"

"It means I'm not totally ignorant of all those unspoken innuendos that were being bantered around the country club tonight. Do you really think I'm so dumb that I don't know what those old coots were thinking?"

Bryce released her to lean back against the door, arms crossed over his chest and an infuriating grin on his face. "What were those old coots thinking?"

She imitated his stance against the footboard of the bed. "They were thinking you'd pulled a mighty slick deal. A bed partner and a rich one to boot."

"Again you amaze me, Mrs. Powell. Not forty-eight hours ago, you were willing to give every appearance of using your money to buy what you wanted."

Marlie stiffened. "That wasn't how I meant to use my money."

"Nevertheless, that's how it would appear to those old coots you're worried about. For appearance sake, I'm kindly refusing your generous offer, Marlie. The reason for this marriage has nothing to do with monetary gain. I want everyone, including Ryan, to realize that."

Oh, he was a stubborn man. And a clever one. He could twist Marlie's good intentions into things of disgrace, leaving her thoroughly confused with whether he was right or wrong. A branch of Stynhearst in Sunnydale would benefit more than herself. Wouldn't it?

"Are you ready for bed?" Bryce asked, shocking her out of her brooding.

"I'm not sleeping with you, Bryce," she grated.

"Yes, you are," he contradicted her gently. "Appearances, remember, Marlie? Ryan would expect us to share a bed."

Marlie's hands became embarrassingly unrestrained, flopping and twisting in agitation while some inward demon turned loose a herd of butterflies in her stomach. She couldn't sleep with Bryce. "Speaking of Ryan," she said nervously, "it's time I put him to bed." Bryce didn't move away from the door, and she wondered if she had the strength and ability to mow him down if he decided to make a stand in the doorway.

Apparently that was his idea. He didn't move. He smiled a lot, but he didn't move. "Ryan's been taken care of," he assured her kindly.

"You didn't take him back to Mrs. Cobb, did you?" she demanded, not knowing whether to hope he did or didn't.

Bryce shook his head. "He's in bed, hopefully asleep by now."

"He allowed you to put him to bed?" she asked suspiciously.

"Allowed isn't exactly the word I'd use. Let's say I won the honor."

"Battling Baboons?"

He nodded.

"I can't imagine you approving, much less encouraging your son to gamble, Bryce."

"Why not? Winning each unwilling concession from my son is proving to be an excellent objective lesson. A couple more heavy losses should cure him of gambling fever forever."

He came away from the door and started for her. Marlie backpedaled around the bed and as far as the wall behind her would allow. She squeezed her eyes shut and waited fatalistically for the first onslaught of Bryce's resolve-ravaging kisses. He took her shoulders into his big hands, but the kisses were stalled by words that did just as much damage.

"I would have come to you sooner, dear," he whispered. "But by the time Ryan had brushed, scrubbed, 'pajamaed' and prayed for blessings on each individual member of the L.A. Dodgers' ball team, we ran overtime in the bedtime ritual."

Marlie didn't open her eyes, but something between a snort and a giggle broke the tension. "You were subjected to the infamous stall treatment. In the event of a stock-market decline, Ryan feels it his duty to pray for all the brokerage firms in the country."

Warm hands traveled across her shoulders and up the sides of her neck. His thumbs massaged the sensitive skin below her ears, sending a shower of giddy chills cascading over her flesh.

"You've done a good job teaching my son sound principles and good habits, Marlie. Too many parents don't take the time to instruct their children in the basics."

Her arms ended up around Bryce's waist, her head leaning against his chest. "I told you that I did my best, Bryce, so you needn't act so surprised by Ryan's willingness to ask God for blessings. I wanted Ryan to have every advantage in life, so of course I wouldn't neglect the most important source."

Those marauding lips were working their way across her cheek. "And do you pray for yourself, Marlie?" he asked the softness beneath his lips.

"Naturally," she murmured back. "I've been keeping God quite entertained the last few days with some outrageous requests."

Bryce grinned against the silky crown of her hair. "Please don't take this as egotistically as it may sound, but did you stop to consider that maybe I'm the answer to your prayers?" he asked lightly, pushing her robe off her shoulders.

That sounded highly egotistical to her indeed, but at the moment she didn't care. She didn't care for several more minutes while Bryce's hands and lips roamed over her. She began caring when he pressed her against the wall and those lovely hands and lips became more hot and demanding. When his hands slipped lower, lower than the sensitive breasts he had fondled with loving intent, she began to panic. His fingers were sneaking under the elastic of tap pants, exploring the area that Marlie knew from female gossip that men were wont to explore.

Until this moment, Marlie had not associated that intimate exploration of a man's fingers in or around her own body, and she saw the unfamiliar experience as frightfully committing. She tried to push him away, then tried to capture all eight hands that the man had suddenly grown. He responded to her by attempting to deepen the kiss.

Trapped. Marlie felt the tentacles of fear winding their way through her body. Bryce wanted to take everything from her. Everything. Would she allow that for the glory of a moment's pleasure? "No," she shouted, and giving him one final shove that should have sent him through the window.

Bryce was fast on his feet. He caught his balance, then turned on Marlie with an almost comical combination of frustrated and incredulous expressions on his passion-hot face. "What in the Sam Hill is wrong with you, woman?" he roared. "You act like a blasted virgin."

Marlie flung herself across the room and whipped up the pillows and blanket that Bryce had brought upstairs with him. "I am a blasted virgin," she shouted back. "And I'd rather be scalped with a dull knife than to let you take one more irretrievable thing away from me."

"You're lying," he accused her hopefully. But he knew she wasn't. She had allowed him close enough in the past few minutes for him to determine that her claim to virginity was a definite possibility. He didn't know whether to laugh or cry.

Cry, he decided a moment later as he saw what she intended to do with those pillows. A wall was going up right down the center of the bed. He knew, but just for the record he thought he might as well ask, "What do you think you're doing?"

Marlie stopped her bed preparations to glare at him. "Personally, I don't care whether you sleep on the sofa, in the car or on a tree limb. But if you insist on sleeping in my bed, I'll at least fix it so you stay on your side."

He pointed at the wall of pillows accusingly. "And just what am I supposed to tell my son that ridiculous big lump under the covers is?"

"Tell him it's your ego, dear," she suggested sweetly. "I'm sure it would take up at least this much room."

Marlie climbed into the bed, pulled the sheet up to her chin and shut out the bedside lamp on her side. Bryce frowned and said, "When I married you, I didn't bargain for..." He stopped. He might as well have, for Marlie had shut him out when she shut off the light. He didn't know what he would have said to her anyway, for he hadn't known what he had bargained for when he married her. Not nearly all of it.

A virgin. No wonder she fell to pieces on him a few minutes ago. He'd gone at her like a love-starved gorilla. Sighing, he got undressed and slid under the pink satin sheet that smelled like Marlie. This just wasn't turning out the way he had planned it. Marlie was supposed to have been a sophisticated woman of sexual experience. He was supposed to put on a convincing charade of marital bliss for his son's peace of mind, plus collect a little pleasure and give a little pleasure in the marriage bed in the meantime.

A virgin. To him, it sounded almost synonymous with *commitment,* and he wasn't certain he could or even wanted to handle that. His own lack of responsibility still haunted him; all the what ifs and maybes that went with a failure one couldn't accept. He had wanted to save his marriage, to recapture his and Janette's once-shared love, but too much horror interfaced the union, too many crippling inadequacies weakened their bond. Helplessly, he had watched one more person he loved pass beyond his reach. Janette's despondency had grown until she had finally ended her torment one night by taking her life.

For months, Bryce had mourned his loss. Mourning drifted into a self-despising punishment for failure. He had tried and found himself guilty of failing as a husband, guilty for not being strong enough to pull his wife back from that black abyss of depression.

Now that wall of insecurity was rising up against him again. Why couldn't Marlie have kept this marriage arrangement simple? Why did she have to put him to a test that he already knew he was doomed to fail?

He raised onto his clbow and peeked over the feather wall at his sleeping wife. Her spectacular body outlined under the sheet obliterated rational considerations. He wanted her. He wanted her to want him. Whoever had thought up the philosophy of mind over matter had been crazy, or else he'd never had a woman as desirable as Marlie in bed with him.

Bryce rolled over onto his back and stared at the ceiling. Hour after hour passed with those treacherous pillows prodding and poking him where it hurt most—his pride. He never would have agreed to allow the erected barrier had he known the agony it would bring.

Or *had* he agreed? He couldn't remember. Later he would take the time to figure it out. Right now he had a score to even.

The sun had taken its sweet time climbing the hills of Sunnydale. When it tentatively peeked into the bedroom window, Bryce threw off the sheet muttering, "It's about time." Wearing his cranky-in-the-morning frown and little else, he walked around the bed to where his wife reposed in blissful, innocent slumber. A sound whack on her bottom brought her yelping straight up in bed.

"Good morning, Mrs. Powell," he said sweetly. "Did you and your plump buddies sleep cozy last night?"

"Ugh!" Marlie flopped back and pulled the sheet over her head.

Bryce planted his legs apart, holding his upper torso stiff-armed on the mattress as he loomed over her. "No? Good. What's for breakfast?"

"Call the café and ask Katy," came the muffled reply.

"Now, now. You don't intend to shirk *all* your wifely duties, do you?"

The sheet crept past her nose, displaying murderous green eyes. "I'd probably get off with a plea of insanity, you know."

Bryce smiled, feeling much better just knowing that she was in as equally bad shape as he. "I don't mind making love to a nut case." He bent down and nuzzled the side of her neck. "If you'd quit strangling yourself with that sheet, I'd show you," he murmured.

"No thanks," she snapped. Her hands exploded out from beneath the sheet, meaning to shove him away, but her fingers tangled in the springy curls on his chest and the skin beneath them felt warm and inviting. She did push, but she didn't put much muscle into it.

Bryce's lips descended to the point of contact when a banging on the bedroom door sent them careening off course. He whipped around and glared at the offending portal as if it had just done something awful to him.

Marlie sighed. "Ah, that would be Ryan. He's demonstrating one of the joys of parenthood that you were so anxious to sample."

"I'll wring his neck."

"No, you won't. You'll let him in." When Bryce straightened, she got a full, eye-popping front view of what she'd been handling with such carelessness a moment before. She gasped, then hissed, "Put a robe on, for heaven's sake."

"Why?" he teased unmercifully. "I doubt my manly physique will bother Ryan nearly as much as it seems to bother you." When he couldn't tell where Marlie's pink face ended and the pink sheet began, he had mercy on her, smirking as he shoved his arms into the sleeves of the robe he had dug out from a box in his apartment.

*  *  *

Breakfast, which could only be called that if one possessed a good imagination or a charitable nature, consisted of a glass of hot orange juice and a half-thawed toasted waffle mercifully drowned in maple syrup.

Bryce viewed his wife's culinary efforts with a dubious eye. The orange juice purely piqued his curiosity. "Why is the juice steaming, Marlie?"

"You should have seen it before I added the hot water."

"Didn't you read the instructions on the can?"

"I know how to mix frozen orange juice, Bryce. I wouldn't have had to use hot water if you'd told me last night that you expected me to be a short-order cook this morning."

Bryce ate the waffle to the point where he figured he'd ruin his teeth if he tried to finish it. Ryan, he noticed, smirked a lot and fixed his own waffle. With the ordeal over, Bryce pushed away from the table, and for the benefit of his son, walked over to Marlie for a goodbye kiss.

Marlie complied, knowing they were keeping up appearances. The taste of maple syrup clung to Bryce's lips, but she knew her husband needed no extra sweetener to make his kisses appealing. He smelled wonderful and he looked darn good in his open-necked oxford shirt and navy sports jacket. If he wasn't a blackmailing jerk, she wouldn't even try to deny her attraction to him.

But a woman had to have some level of standard, and the Rex Kanes and the Bryce Powells of this cruel world were below it. She spent the day alternately worrying about the former and resenting the later until she was tense and irritable and ready to take Ryan's head off at the least offence. A night of pretend sleep could do that to a person.

"You're cross, Aunt Marlie," Ryan informed her after beating her at another video game. "I think you need a nap."

Marlie nodded in agreement, and after going over all the precautions against intruders, she stretched out on the sofa and was asleep before Ryan could decide what game to play solo.

The morning stretched into the afternoon, and Aunt Marlie showed no signs of awakening. Ryan was getting restless with boredom. Even pestering Mr. Powell would have been preferable to the quietness of the lonely apartment. Diversion finally came with the tinkling of familiar bells on the street outside the apartments.

"The ice-cream man," the little boy whispered gleefully. He ran quietly up the stairs to collect his money and stopped at the dining room table for the house keys. He wasn't sneaking out, he assured himself as he slipped out the front door. This wasn't like the time he'd sneaked to the alley at midnight to put that dead kitty in Mr. Powell's trash can. It was broad daylight outside, and the ice-cream man wasn't in the alley.

While Ryan was deliberating over Bubble Gum Delight and Rocky Road Mocha, his attention was caught by a car so similar to Mr. Powell's, that the boy feared for a moment that he had been caught red-handed. The maroon car stopped several yards away, and through the tinted glass Ryan could distinguish only that the male driving had a beard and was wearing a baseball hat and dark glasses.

Since the man wasn't Mr. Powell and Ryan hadn't been caught after all, the child dismissed the stranger as unimportant and went about selecting and paying for his ice cream.

Back in the kitchen, he quickly devoured the whole cone, buried the messy napkin deep in the trash, then carefully washed his hands and face.

Feeling slightly smug and very grown-up, Ryan went back to his video game with his beloved Aunt Marlie none the wiser.

Marlie awakened a little after five o'clock and went immediately into a panic. Five o'clock, and not a decent thing in the house for dinner. The beast would expect to be fed, wouldn't he? She grabbed her apartment keys and Ryan's hand and literally ran to the market. Uncaring at this point of whether or not the *Sunnydale Herald* or the local grapevine had reported the news of her innocence, she swept past the checkout lady and down the aisles, grabbing produce and meat and stacking them into Ryan's arms.

The lady had rung up the purchases and informed Marlie of the total before Marlie finally stopped to think. She didn't have one cent on her. Bryce still had her purse, and she rarely stuffed her pockets with money, though she could have.

Before she'd fled L.A., Marlie had stopped by her bank and connived her banker into believing she needed an inordinately large amount of cash for a business transaction. Much of that cash was still in a dirty old gym bag under her bed at the apartment. But that didn't solve her problem now, did it?

The dismay on her face telegraphed her problem to the checkout lady, who smiled benignly and said, "That's all right, Mrs. Powell. Bryce can pay me later."

The checkout lady's acknowledgment of Marlie's marital status hardly registered as she walked red-faced from the store. And Marlie's disgrace knew no end. Once home, everything in the kitchen went wrong. The dining room table, however, looked quite nice when she finally called Bryce and Ryan into the dining room.

Marlie served the salad, and as she was leaving the room to fetch the dressing, she caught Bryce's facetious, and unwise, remark. "Be warned, Ryan. This is a psychological trick that women play on men. They set the table with bone china and linen napkins, then serve us salad and we're supposed to believe it's a real meal."

Marlie's lips tightened grimly. She'd show him a real meal. She brought in his steak, flopped it onto his bone china plate, and said sweetly, "I didn't know how you like it, so I cooked it all three ways."

Bryce stared at the contents of his plate a full minute, trying to decide what it was, or used to be.

"It's a steak," Ryan offered, smirking.

Bryce nodded and picked up his knife and fork. Marlie had said there was a perfect layer of meat somewhere between the blood and ashes. He was determined to find it. And praise it. It was the least he could do to get this marriage business off on the right foot.

After martyring himself at the table, Bryce herded his little family into the living room. He saw that Ryan was prepared to pretend that Bryce's presence in this home was of no more consequence than the elephant's foot umbrella stand, which, for some obscure reason, Marlie had purchased to grace the corner of the room. Predicting such a reception from Ryan, Bryce had come prepared. He hauled out a chess set from his satchel and seated himself on the carpet.

As he had hoped, the lure of the handsome ivory pieces proved too much for the curious little boy and he was soon squatting on the other side of the board.

"I'll take on all comers," Bryce said after the pieces were arranged and several silent moments had passed.

"I haven't learned to play yet," the child said with a touch of reluctant yearning.

"The best way to learn is to play."

Ryan shook his head. "I'd rather watch," he stated firmly, though the disappointment was obvious.

"You have an opponent in mind for me?" Bryce asked.

Ryan looked over his shoulder. Aunt Marlie sat in her recliner, her nose buried in a magazine. "Aunt Marlie will play," he volunteered.

Aunt Marlie visibly stiffened, but did not emerge from the magazine to take up the challenge. "Ryan, can't you see your aunt is terribly busy at the moment?" Bryce asked.

Ryan looked again, then turned his puzzled blue eyes back to Bryce. Feeling like the jerk he was accused of being, Bryce explained in a voice that was the soul of compassion, "She's pouting, Ryan. Your Aunt Marlie has many grievances to bear and she's wisely using this otherwise useless rainy night to bemoan life's miserable circumstances that have brought her down to this lowly state."

As Bryce had hoped, Ryan was having a difficult time catching the full impact of the insults. Marlie was hanging on his every word... and no doubt wishing the hapless magazine being twisted beneath her hands could be replaced with his neck. Bryce chuckled; he wasn't finished with her yet. "Besides that, Ryan, she's a chicken."

Marlie lowered the magazine and stared at him. Ryan puffed up with indignation on her behalf. "Not my Aunt Marlie. She's not afraid of anything."

"I'm sorry, but that's not true. I discovered just last night that she's reluctant to try anything new." He lowered his gaze and wagged his head sadly. "I'm not sure what she feels her inadequacies are, but they leave her positively... frigid."

The recliner slammed to an upright position. A moment later he was looking at ten, cute little toes resting on the edge of the chessboard. His eyes slowly wandered up the long length of her thighs, visually caressed their sweet junction, continued upward to where her folded arms pushed the swell of her breasts into admirable relief and finished the tour at her mouth, which pouted adorably, whether she'd admit it or not.

"Tell him you aren't frigid, Aunt Marlie," Ryan demanded.

"What Mr. Powell isn't telling you, Ryan, is that I just wasn't interested in the game he wanted to play last night."

"I wouldn't insult your intelligence, Ryan, by stating the obvious. I was just explaining to you that your Aunt Marlie fears losing something she's never risked before, too much to shake her inhibitions."

"White or black, Mr. Powell?" she asked icily, dropping down onto the carpet.

"Lady's choice, Mrs. Powell."

Marlie and Bryce took out many of their frustrations for one another at the chessboard that evening. When the floor became too hard against Marlie's bottom, they moved the game to the dining room table, which proved to be a tactical error on her part. Bryce's bare foot persisted in trying to climb her shin en route to her lap. Finally she waylaid its attempt by coyly smoothing her palm over his calf, bared by skimpy running shorts, until she found a thick crop of hair, grasped a handful and gave it a good tweak. Bryce straightened in his chair with a startled yelp. Once peace was restored to the dining room—Bryce having had Ryan crawl around under the table looking for the monster who had attacked him—everyone got back to uninterrupted concentration on the game.

An equal number of chessmen had retired to the sidelines at either end of the board when the game was called, for Ryan's bedtime. The child dragged his feet all the way up the stairs, demanding scout's honor promises that they wouldn't continue the game until he could watch. The promises were given, but it left the promisers in a terrible lurch.

Marlie walked back down the stairs, aware of Bryce dogging her every step. What was she supposed to do with him for the next couple of hours? She quickly canceled the dumb question, knowing all too well what a wife was supposed to do with her husband after the kids were put to bed. None of that applied to her unorthodox situation, did it?

Conversation. Yes, that was an innocuous solution to the problem. They could surely think up enough topics that interested them both. While she was wracking her brain for the perfect conversational gambit, Bryce stepped in and took over—as usual.

"You play a good game of chess. Who taught you to play?" he asked.

"Benny."

"Who's Benny?"

"My chauffeur."

"Of course. Did you let Benny teach you any other games?"

"Only ones that I was sure I could win." She turned to face him, sighing in exasperation. "You have a dirty mind, Mr. Powell. I acknowledge the advantage that gives you, and don't even pretend that I could match your finesse in the bedroom. Maybe I do value winning too much to take risks. But at the risk of being accused of bemoaning my grievances again, I will tell you that I'm already losing about all I can stand to lose." She blinked away a few infuriating tears, took a breath and concluded with, "Now, do we change the subject, or do I go find a book to read?"

"Change the subject," Bryce said soberly.

She nodded agreement, thought a moment, then commented, "Bringing out the chessboard was a clever move on your part. Ryan gobbles up a new challenge like it's candy."

Bryce stretched out on the living room floor again, way closer to Marlie's legs than she thought necessary when the whole room was at his disposal. He didn't seem to notice, or mind, that his proximity bothered her as he answered, "I thought that might do the trick. Still, chess is a complicated game for a six-year-old."

She drew her legs up under her, hoping to make herself a small target against his predatory gaze. "For many six-year-olds, maybe, but not Ryan."

Bryce nodded, chuckling. "He told me he had a problem with his intelligence."

"Some problem. I had Ryan tested. He has a near perfect auditory and visual memory. The next time you get out the chessboard, ask him what he remembers learning about the game from the last time we played. I'd bet money that he can duplicate each move we made tonight, plus repeat verbatim your explanations for making those moves."

Bryce shook his head, plainly awed by his son. "Poor kid," he said wryly. Marlie surprised him by taking his remark seriously.

"Yes. Poor kid. Ryan's extraordinary intellect leaves him socially isolated from the average six-year-old who still puts his shoes on the wrong feet and occasionally wears his T-shirt backward."

"So are you Ryan's playmate, Marlie? Is that why he's so attached to you?"

"Partly. I'd like to think that Ryan and I are involved with one another on a deeper, more emotional level, as well." Marlie went on to tell Bryce about the son whose companionship he'd been denied for four and a half years. The minutes ticked by slowly, but were made tolerable by conversing on a topic that each loved. It didn't squelch their physical awareness of one another, but it helped....

Thus began the routine that would provide chilling diversion for the next four, rainy miserable nights. Each evening, Bryce would join Ryan and Marlie at the dinner table where Bryce stoically ignored Marlie's attempts to poison him with her cooking. After clearing the table, the chess-board was brought out, where Marlie taught him the humble art of losing, while his son cheered the opposition on to victory.

The time between Ryan's bedtime and the dreaded witching hour held their own unsettling predicaments. But it was after midnight that the true horror began.

Bryce would enter the upstair's torture chamber, strip to the buff, then manfully stretch himself on the rack of forced celibacy. That he was aware that his beautiful wife, who preferred the company of goose feathers to that of her husband, was sliding two gorgeous legs between his sheets on the other side of the Iron Curtain, made the grueling test of self-control and perseverance even more painful.

Yet, if Bryce thought he suffered alone, he was mistaken. Marlie suffered in the same elemental ways because Bryce made certain that she did. There was nothing mystical in what the man did. He simply possessed an erotic earthiness that pulled human nature up by the roots, exposing raw desire and need. When Marlie looked at him, she knew exactly what she wanted, if not exactly why.

Or maybe she did know why. She was a normal, healthy woman with the usual hormones that could plague a person at the most inconvenient times. When a true-to-life statue of a Greek god did a strip show for her in their bedroom, she responded. She'd really be worried about what kind of psychological effect Rex had had on her if she didn't respond to Bryce's blatant sexuality.

So for four stormy nights, Marlie shared Bryce's rack of forced celibacy, acutely aware of its discomfort, but ignorance spared her the full power of its misery.

The end of the week provided a new diversion. The sun popped up into a cobalt sky to shine innocently down on a water-logged Sunnydale, as if its conspicuous absence hadn't frazzled the nerves of the residents. Marlie was so thrilled with the change in weather that she tore off her shoes and socks, encouraged Ryan to do the same, and both splashed in the puddles of Pothole Alley.

When the fun wore off, they fetched the ball and bat and had a practice session, while Marlie mentally planned dinner.

While Marlie was tossing softballs to Ryan and plotting a ghastly gastronomical fate for Bryce, the man in question returned home from a round of victory drinks at the pub. His ball team, the Sunnydale Pirates, had won their game, and frankly, Bryce couldn't have cared less. He had sat there in his booth, nursing a drink that he hadn't wanted and thinking about his wife's body, which he did want. He'd left the pub early, unable to bear the thought of his teammates seeing him cry in his beer.

Now he trudged upstairs to shower, shave and change his clothes. Twenty minutes later he was ready to face another night of being driven crazy by thoughts of the woman who tempted him like a feast spread on a beggar's table.

Hearing laughter coming from the backyard, Bryce decided to torture himself again by watching Marlie and his son play. He slid open the sliding-glass door of the bedroom balcony and walked out, preparing to have his heart slam-dunked. They were having a two-man practice session of softball in the yard.

Nope, Bryce corrected himself, one of them was definitely not male. No masculine hips could ever grace the seat of a pair of cutoff jeans the way this woman's did. Marlie hefted her bat and struck a pose against the sunset that silhouetted every tantalizing curve of her body. And just to make certain Bryce's blood pressure shot through the roof, she augmented her athletic posture with an unorthodox wiggle of her backside. He could have wept with the pity of allowing all that physical exertion to go to waste. "She's turning me into a sex maniac," he muttered disparagingly. But before he had a chance to make a brilliant play for his future lover, he had to snap back to reality and make a brilliant play for the softball headed straight for Mrs. Cobb's sliding-glass door behind him. He reached out and caught it barehanded in the nick of time. From the improvised ball field, two faces stared up at him, one startled, the other frightened but mutinous. With one half-dead brain cell,

Bryce could have figured out who had thrown the wildly aimed ball.

Marlie looked at Ryan. She knew for a fact that that wild ball was an accident, but from the smug look on her nephew's face, she'd never prove it. "I know Ryan didn't mean to lose control of the ball, Bryce," she called up to the balcony.

Bryce cocked his arm and threw the ball clear to the hedges edging the alley. "Practice your outfielding, Ryan," he said calmly. Once the boy had warily trotted off, Bryce draped himself over the balcony railing and picked up his conversation with Marlie, but surprised her with its content.

"Did you know that I wake up an hour before the alarm goes off in the morning just so I can watch you sleep?"

Marlie's attention snapped back from Ryan grappling in the hedges for the ball to the man serenading her with sensual nonsense from the balcony. Somehow during the past three days, she had almost convinced herself that his sexual attraction was a passing fancy and could be dealt with in a pragmatic manner. As for herself, the pillows hadn't worked, not the way she'd planned.

She looked at the man on the balcony, and the words she longed to say to him silently telegraphed themselves via her wide green eyes: Did you know that I lie awake at night an extra hour just to listen to your breathing beside me? Did you know that my hands tremble with the need to touch you? Knowing you're so close, Bryce, yet more than a barrier of pillows away, hurts.

She turned away from him, hiding her despair.

But Bryce had seen enough. He vaulted the balcony rail, the rain-softened earth and the flex of his knees absorbing the shock of the eight-foot drop, but he didn't even notice. He landed on his feet and just kept on going until he was panting at the heels of his body's desire.

"You're holding the bat wrong, honey," he said, reaching out to grasp her shoulders from behind, before she was even aware he was close.

"Oh," she gasped. She swung the bat. Bryce ducked. Then somehow they ended up in each other's arms, their lips

fused with longing. Bryce drew her hard against him, and
Marlie reached up on the tips of her toes, seeking the intimate clasp that would relieve the ache in untouched places.
She wanted to surround the heat and the strength of his desire that nudged against her in the most elemental way of
woman. She wanted…oh, she wanted everything. But how
did a woman say yes after saying no for so long?

Bryce finally eased them apart. "Do you know what
amazes me about you?" he asked, his breath ragged as he
rested his forehead against hers.

"I should imagine quite a lot," she said dryly.

Bryce chuckled. "Yes, a lot. But at the top of the list is
how you could kiss a man like that and remain chaste. Don't
the men in California have any feelings?"

Marlie shrugged. "I guess most of them do. The one I
managed to fall in love with didn't."

Bryce could tell the subject was turning sour. Before he
could change it, Ryan was shoving his belligerent little face
between them.

"Are we going to play ball or not?" he demanded.

"We're going to play ball," Marlie confirmed stoutly.

"After I show you how to hold the bat properly," Bryce
interjected. "Right, dear?"

She nodded.

Mistake! Marlie knew it the moment Bryce inferred that
she needed to tighten up her batting stance—though he did
whisper in her ear that he found her form inspiring—and she
had fallen for it like a nincompoop.

No matter how carefully she followed his instructions for
remedying her stance, something wasn't quite right. Naturally, he had to precisely align the incorrect parts of her
anatomy, which required having his hands all over her. Well,
not all over her, she amended ruefully. A couple of places
felt woefully neglected.

By the time Bryce had improved her position they were
both breathing funny again, and swinging a bat was the last
thing on their minds. All that saved their reputations was
Ryan standing a few yards away, diligently watching for one
false move.

Needing to be away from Bryce's disturbing maleness, Marlie took a swing at one of Ryan's crazily tossed balls and surprised all of them by knocking it over the hedge and into the alley. She handed the bat to Bryce, hastily saying, "You were so right about correcting my stance. It's worked wonders." She smiled ruefully. "Now I'll see what wonders I can perform for dinner."

Bryce frantically shook his head. "This evening's too nice to sp—" He smoothly corrected his tactless "spoil" without Marlie the wiser. "—Spend in a hot kitchen. We'll eat out."

Even Ryan smiled at the cheerful news and volunteered to put away the ball equipment.

# Eight

That night, back in the torture chamber, Bryce lay upon his bed of nails while good old-fashioned lust worked its way through his system like Drano. He'd thought and thought, but there seemed to be but one solution to his problem. Marlie may kill him and the whole thing would be over, but tonight he was going to arrange the marital bed to his advantage.

He threw off the sheet, jackknifed out of bed and snapped on the bedside lamp. Marlie, he saw, was sitting up in bed at attention, too, with the sheet grasped under her chin. He yanked the sheet away from her to expose those ornery pillows.

"The marriage vows I took stated until death do us part. They said nothing about allowing pillows to part us. So—" he gathered the offending items "—the pillows go."

And they went—right out the window. Bryce slammed the window shut and dusted his hands together as if relieved to have that piece of nasty business over. Then he began to pace, his voice that of a commando leader addressing his troops. "The marriage vows also stated 'for better or worse.' Well, from now on we're going to deal with the worse until it gets better. Maybe it's sinful to take a woman while leaving the emotional commitment unsettled. I don't know. What I do know is that I want you. We're legally married, and I have to play the hand that's been dealt to me, as best I can. When you're ready to do the same, let me know.''

Having said his piece he climbed back into bed, pulled the sheet up and snapped off the light.

Marlie's eyes widened incredulously. That was it? He rises up to do battle for her favors, armored in nothing but bronzed skin, armed with nothing but hot air, and he expects her to *let him know?*

She'd let him know, all right. And she'd do it with fewer words and less theatrics. ''I'm ready,'' she said in a calm, clear voice.

A gusty breath exploded from across the bed. Thankfully, Bryce moved a lot faster than he lectured, or Marlie might have changed her mind. Or maybe she wouldn't have. She was out of her mind, anyway. But this night was just for her, partly because she was curious about all the longings Bryce inspired, and partly because...because...

Marlie ran out of time and excuses just as Bryce took her into his arms. He lay his head upon her breast, his breath coming rapidly like a runner crossing the finishing line. She threaded her fingers through his hair, tugging his head up until she could see the moonlight silvering his eyes.

''I'm not sure I like you well enough to be doing this with you, Powell,'' she whispered flippantly.

''I'll help you make up your mind,'' he promised. ''You're going to love making love, Marlie. It's a lot more fun—and easier—than...say...making dinner.''

He was teasing her, and Marlie was grateful. It relieved much of the pressure of taking that final step that could never be retraced. ''That's good to hear. Do you know how difficult it is to burn a hot dog when you're cooking it in boiling water?''

Bryce chuckled, resting his forehead against hers, noses touching. ''I knew that had to be deliberate,'' he accused her lightly. Then, gently he added in the same breath against her lips, ''Don't be afraid, Marlie. Where we're going, we'll go together. It's a trip up to the stars, and coming down is finding a perfect air current that brings you gently back to earth."

She wrapped her arms around his neck. "I may need a few flight instructions."

"It just so happens..." His words dissolved against her lips in a quick kiss before he ducked beneath the sheet. "First we have to light the runway," he explained, backing his way down the length of her body, destroying her composure with a string of damp kisses that landed on each peak and every valley of significance from her chin to her toes.

Marlie hummed with tension, certain that he was producing enough current to light up Pittsburgh. "I think I'm glowing, Bryce," she wheezed. But he wasn't satisfied yet. He picked up one foot in each hand, and with the tips of his fingers did a maddening little dance on her insteps. She sucked in her breath, feeling the sensations deep inside. When he replaced his fingers with his lips, his smile left its imprint upon her arches before he moved onward.

That devilish tongue, which could utter words to whip her senses into a frenzy, could also torment in the mute mode. It wound its way up her shin, made a couple of laps around her kneecap, traversed her thigh, then pressed over the quivering flesh of her stomach that lay beneath the satin of her camisole top. Marlie thought she'd surely blast off without him when he paid tribute with a hot, gusty kiss to the center front appliquéd rose on her tap pants.

Bryce laughed, a joyous musical of delight. "Now you're glowing, Marlie," he intoned lightly.

"So I am," she said, panting. "What's next?"

"Now we uncover the...huh..."

"Thrusters?" She guessed when he hesitated. She ran her hands down his flanks, relishing the little moan she incited. "Yours seem to be exposed already."

"Darling, they've been revved up for this moment ever since I met you in the alley a week ago," he groaned. His fingers traced the deep V edges of her pants. "Can we get rid of this?" He didn't wait for permission, but pulled the tiny straps of her top down her shoulders, over her breasts and bunched it with the bottoms. One sweep of his hand left

Marlie as exposed to the human eye as when Nanny Jane
had bathed her as a toddler.

The moments that followed became breathtakingly individual. Mission control moved from Marlie's mind to her
heart, then to the heart of her gender. Each drugging kiss,
each probing touch, prepared her for the journey Bryce had
promised. The stars that had seemed too impossible to reach
came closer and shimmered with a light that diffused itself
inside her.

When Bryce pressed the union, Marlie opened to him,
inviting him to take her. And he did. With the tender love of
his body, he tore away the barrier of emotional agony of the
days past as he tore away the physical barrier that brought
her agony for but a moment.

Then the stars were hers. She shared them with her lover,
and felt the touch of an angel's wings. The moments blurred
until time had no meaning and space was what could be
filled with blissful stardust. The free-fall to earth was as
gentle and peaceful as Bryce had promised, and when she
opened her eyes, he was with her, holding her safely in his
arms.

Bryce tenderly kissed away the tracks of tears on Marlie's
cheeks. He kneaded the soft breast beneath his hand and felt
the pounding rhythm of her heart slowing as she touched
ground. He sighed in relief, knowing that she had found
satisfaction. But had she been where he had gone? With
awestruck senses, he realized that her sweet, innocent flesh
had surrounded him, raised him up and transported him to
a place he'd never been.

Lethargy fused the muscles in Marlie's body. Seeing the
question in Bryce's eyes, the concern etched into his face,
she made the effort and raised an arm, slowly tracing the
solemn lips and worried brow of the man hovering above
her. She smiled for him. "I've just come back from frolick-
ing in stardust with the angels," she whispered.

The worry lines transformed into two dimples that
dropped the stars back into her eyes.

It took Bryce less than a week to determine that the wisdom of the ages applied to him as well as the rest of hu-

manity: a satisfying sex life did not take the edge off his remaining anxieties. If anything, it made it worse.

At night he could hold Marlie in his arms and pretend that the reasons she was there didn't matter. But the cold, gray dawn came armed with truth. Reality was a woman who responded to him like a dream in the night, but by day, erected a barricade against him more formidable than any feather pillow had represented. Reality was a little boy who loved his Aunt Marlie and plotted the elimination of all competition trying to separate the two of them.

Bryce knew that Marlie was the key to change, but how was he to make her give over what he wanted? In fairness, he had to admit that she was doing what she could to nudge Ryan in his direction. In fairness, he had to admit that he didn't blame her for guarding her emotions. He was doing the same himself. He wanted answers to his problems now, and as usual, he would have to go to Marlie to get them.

He searched for and found her on the patio. She wasn't alone, for Ryan had found her first. His son was hunched protectively over his aunt, patting her back and murmuring words that Bryce couldn't hear. He eased the sliding door open an inch and concealed himself behind the curtain. As he listened he got some of the answers he was seeking. They pelted him like the debris of an unexpected landslide.

"Don't cry, Aunt Marlie," Ryan murmured tearfully. "I love you. Please, don't cry."

Thinking she was alone on the patio, Marlie straightened abruptly. She hastily wiped away the tears and gave the child her brightest, if most insincere smile. "Good morning, honey. I love you, too, and I'm not crying. I thought I'd just catch a bit of the cool morning air before fixing breakfast."

"Aunt Marlie, you're telling a fib," he said, patting her damp cheeks. "You're not happy, are you?"

Marlie gulped. Oh, Ryan, you see too much, and I hate telling you fibs. "Of course I'm happy. I'm always happy when I'm with you."

"But not him," Ryan spat. "Does he make you homesick?"

Homesick? Marlie wondered. Actually, she was sick of home. Bryce's home. This home that wasn't hers. She was sick of everything falling apart in her life and feeling sorry for herself because it did. She had a crazed ex-fiancé trailing her. She was losing her sweet Ryan. And she had become a slave to her passions, thanks to her uncommitted husband.

Lovemaking with Bryce had become a nightly indulgence that she hated to love. Hated, because for the first three nights they'd "indulged," she had waited, in vain, to hear some words that would warm her heart as well as her body. Yes, he'd tell her that she was beautiful and sexy and responsive. But was that it? Was she just an ornamental bed warmer?

For the past two nights, she'd tried eliminating the "responsive" in his list of her attributes, but she'd failed miserably. His sneaky hands unerringly found the places in need of attention and his clever mouth knew tricks to sway her willpower. Her consolation was that she refused to love the man who loved only her body; this much pride she would take to her grave.

"Does he, Aunt Marlie?" Ryan repeated, interrupting her gloomy thoughts. "Does he make you homesick?"

"*He* has a name, Ryan," she said with gentle rebuke. "Please show the respect that I taught you."

"He—I mean, Mr. Powell, said I could call him Dad," Ryan scoffed. "I won't call anyone Dad who's as mean as he is."

"Bryce has treated you mean?" she demanded, aghast.

"Well," the child hedged, scuffing his sneaker over the cobblestones. "Not me. But he does you, or you wouldn't be so sad all the time."

Marlie closed her eyes and almost moaned aloud. What was she doing? Ryan's anger with Bryce on her behalf wouldn't do. Her hopes of visitation rights were going up in smoke before her weepy eyes, plus she couldn't stand the thought of worrying Ryan. She was just going to have to put a happier face on the grudging duties of being a wife to a blackmailer.

"Ryan," she said gently. "Bryce isn't mean to me. Honestly. Maybe you're right. Maybe I'm just a little homesick. I do miss the ocean and the beaches in L.A. But I kind of like Sunnydale, too. The people here are nice, and I think you would like Bryce, too, if you gave him a chance."

Ryan folded his arms over his chest and looked totally unconvinced. He would have to see it to believe it. So Marlie was going to have to see to it that the little guy saw it. Her no-more-tears formula for existing called for a new attitude, and it would start this minute. "How about helping me incinerate the breakfast bacon, honey?" she teased him.

Ryan blinked in surprise, then grinned gamely.

She stood up, wrapped her arm around Ryan's shoulder and headed them toward the patio door. The affectionate gesture was reciprocated with an arm around her waist. "Why don't you hire a cook like we had in L.A., Aunt Marlie?" the child asked earnestly. "You've never cooked before and... well... I don't want to hurt your feelings, but..."

"My cooking stinks," she finished for him. Ryan didn't disagree. She nodded forlornly, knowing this was something else that would have to change. "I don't believe Bryce wants to spend the money for hiring a cook right now, Ryan."

"But you have plenty of money, Aunt Marlie."

"Yes, but Bryce thinks of it as *my* money, not his. I think it's a point of pride with him that he be able to take care of you—us—with the money he earns."

Shaking his head, Ryan reached for the handle of the sliding door. "I think I'd take your money and hire a cook instead of starving to death."

Marlie burst out laughing. "I'm happy to see that you're growing up more practical than macho, darling. We may have to see if we can convince Bryce of your wisdom if my cooking doesn't improve soon."

"If what doesn't improve soon?" Bryce asked, sliding the door open wider.

Marlie looked up, startled. Where had he come from? She smiled at her husband and winked at Ryan. "The weather,

Bryce," she answered. "The mornings are the only fit time to be outside."

He stared at her a long, unnerving moment, then shrugged. Turning toward the kitchen, he called over his shoulder, "What's for breakfast? I'm starved."

She looked at Ryan, and the boy giggled evilly. "Incinerated bacon and gooey scrambled eggs," she called back.

"Great!" Bryce said with unwarranted eagerness. "Just the way I like them."

Marlie put her new attitude into effect that afternoon. She was going to smile and act happy, even if it cost her a nervous breakdown.

To initiate the new Marlie Powell attitude, she chose, with ingenuous enthusiasm, a project. She and Ryan trooped down to the hardware store, purchased a barbecue grill and lugged it back to the patio. Undaunted by the lack of tools, she improvised with a dinner knife, and while Ryan read the assembling instructions, she meticulously knifed four chrome legs into the bottom of the red enamel grill pit.

Because Marlie had always had her protein served ready-cooked on a silver platter, she had to rely heavily on grilling technique propaganda. First, she dumped a whole bag of charcoal into the pit. Next, she doused the little black bricks until they were floating in a sea of starter fluid. "Stand back, Ryan," she ordered, then struck a kitchen match and tossed it into the pit.

*Whooosh!*

Marlie let out a startled yelp as a towering inferno shot into the sky. "Ryan, get the water hose from the side of the building," she cried. But it was too late. Dispiritedly, she saw her brand-new grill being consumed by the conflagration.

While Marlie was experiencing the delights of outdoor cooking, Bryce returned home. Hearing squeals of glee coming from the backyard and thinking it must be another ball practice in session, he slid open the door of the bedroom balcony. He didn't see Ryan around, but Marlie was there. She appeared to be war dancing around some huge ceremonial fire. From the way she wrung her hands, she must have been anticipating a fierce battle.

Sighing, Bryce headed for the patio.

"Marlie," he called just loudly enough to gain her attention. She turned to him, cringing. Her fatalistic frown made him want to take her in his arms and reassure her about such calamities of life. Pity would probably get him a punch in the nose, so he settled for some gentle teasing.

Staring morosely at the unrestrained flaming mass he said, "I don't mean to be critical, dear, but since we've been married, about half the food you've brought to the table has been raw. That's okay, because it wasn't really dangerous if we avoided it. It's when you set off the fire alarms in the kitchen that the situation becomes tense. Now your pyromania has moved outdoors, and if I'm to spare Sunnydale, I think I'd better hire us a cook."

It took everything in Marlie to refrain from leaping into his arms and kissing him breathless. Instead, very reserved, she asked, "You mean that's all I needed to do to get a cook sooner? Burn down the town?"

Marlie's fire in the pit matched the blue flare in Bryce's eyes. He smiled lustfully. "Come here," he ordered gently, pulling Marlie into his embrace. Marlie didn't fight it; she willingly lifted her lips to his. And right before she would have closed her eyes in blissful surrender, she caught a glimpse of what was advancing on Bryce from the rear.

Marlie had forgotten about Ryan, and it was the wrong thing to do to a boy with a vendetta. He was marching toward his nemesis, dragging the water hose, and Marlie didn't need two guesses for what he had in mind.

"No, Ryan," she yelled, then huddled within Bryce's protective bulk, knowing she yelled too late. The boy aimed his weapon, turned the nozzle to full force and blasted Bryce squarely between the shoulder blades.

Ryan's entire assault had lasted mere seconds. Bryce stood perfectly motionless, like a granite statue of a valiant general. It wasn't funny. So why did Marlie have an insane urge to laugh? In the preservation of life, she turned away from the sight of this six-foot-three-inch drowned rat, with metaphorical steam rolling off his broad shoulders.

Not a man to take aggressive rebellion lightly, Bryce turned for a counterattack. Ryan must have understood the look on Bryce's face for he dropped the hose and took to his heels. He was fast, but Bryce was faster. Soon the big man was upon the child and scooping him under one arm.

"Your aunt likes to play with fire, and you like to play with water, huh, Ryan?" he demanded, laughing. He savored the feel of the squirming bundle against him until he reached the hose. Tucking the nozzle into the back waistband of Ryan's jeans, Bryce added, "You two are going to have to learn that one way or another I usually retaliate." Then he turned on the cold, cold water.

Marlie stood a safe distance away and watched her Ryan being psychologically bamboozled by the biggest charmer in the county. Ryan squirmed, kicked...and laughed, as Bryce had his way with the child. Marlie's heart lurched, knowing she was witnessing the beginning of the end of her time with Ryan.

As she quickly wiped away tears that went unnoticed as the two drowned rats came over to face her, Bryce said, "I'll take over the grilling detail under two conditions. Since I don't want food poisoning, natural or otherwise, I'll furnish the meat from my freezer. And Ryan, here, has to eat with a plastic fork at least thirty feet away from me."

The implications of the conditions were clearly understood by the little boy, and he looked quite excited to have this interloper pick up the gauntlet.

Bryce's hamburgers turned out perfect—nice and evenly browned outside, pink and juicy inside. Marlie had to choke hers down, trying to swallow Bryce's smug grin with each bite.

Bryce's smugness lasted right up until bedtime. The chess game did not go in Marlie's favor. How could it when she was pitted against a passion phenomena? Bryce had a way with sexual innuendo that left her gaping at his audacity and Ryan frowning in perplexity. What Bryce's words didn't accomplish, his under-the-table foot tactics did. Before the chess game was over, she was moving *his* chessmen around the board.

The end of the evening was a foregone conclusion. Marlie lost at chess and Bryce won the real game they'd been playing all evening. Marlie couldn't say she was all that disappointed.

Much later, she lay snug against Bryce's side, making lazy circles on his damp chest. "I didn't get a chance to thank you for buying me a cook," she told him drowsily.

Bryce waded through the haze of sleep that obscured his thinking. "Consider her my birthday present to you," he murmured, smiling.

"My birthday isn't until February," she said, disappointment worrying her voice.

Bryce almost laughed. "We won't survive until then, so consider her my birthday present, which is next month." He felt her smile against his shoulder and smiled himself. "I have to warn you, though. Domestic help doesn't grow on trees in Sunnydale. It could take a while to find someone. In the meantime you might ask Mrs. Cobb for a few cooking lessons."

"Hmm... Maybe. But speaking of birthdays, when's Ryan's?"

He frowned at the odd question, then logic gave him an answer. "No, you wouldn't know, would you?"

She shrugged. "I never did find Ryan's birth certificate or any other legal documents stating the details of his birth. Rex claimed he had no idea what happened to those things, so I gave Ryan a birthday to celebrate until we found them."

She moved her hand from Bryce's chest to a small ache at her temple. "Maybe I should have been curious of Ryan's origin right then. Rex said he'd take care of the legal details, and frankly, I was so happy to have Ryan that I pushed the matter aside."

Bryce was beginning to wake up—in several ways. Questions that had bothered his subconscious since finding his son and Marlie now demanded answers. "You told me that your brother had Ryan for a year and a half before the accident. How could you have not known anything about Ryan?"

"Because I hadn't seen Andrew since our parents' funeral. Contact with my brother was limited to a written yearly report of the status of my assets and the interest balance of my trust fund, which, as my legal guardian, he controlled. I didn't know Ryan existed until I took custody of him at his parents' funeral."

Bryce repressed a shudder at her unaffected acceptance of the unemotional relationship she'd shared with her brother. For Pete's sake, Bryce's family was flung over the country, but he still knew when his parents bought a new car, his sister broke a fingernail and his brother's wife had another baby.

He swallowed hard as the significance of Ryan in Marlie's life began to fully register. Ryan wasn't just a bored, rich woman's indulgence. He was all the family Marlie really had.

"Ryan's birthday is the eighteenth of April, Marlie," he said gently.

She snuggled closer, tracing his collarbone with her fingertips. "Was he a good baby?"

"Yes. But he was a handful. Ryan's had that knowing look in his eye since he was a week old. Scared the heck out of Janette and me."

They talked about Ryan until Marlie's voice drifted off in midquestion, and Bryce felt the final sweep of her lashes against his shoulder. Sleep didn't claim him as mercifully. He lay awake a long time, thinking about the child he had finally found and the woman who was losing him.

"Is Ryan ready to go?" Bryce asked from the doorway of the kitchen.

Marlie looked up from the stroganoff she was laboring over. "I sent him to get ready thirty minutes ago." Speaking to Mrs. Cobb behind her, she asked, "Can you spare me a moment?"

"Of course, dear," she said kindly, but with a roll of her eyes aimed at Bryce. "You run along and help Ryan and Bryce." As if it were a magic wand, she waved a wooden spoon at a pot bubbling on the stove. "These noodles still need to cook more."

Marlie nodded, wiped her hands on a damp towel and led the way upstairs. At the bathroom door, she and Bryce halted at the sounds of moaning coming from inside. Marlie opened the door and found Ryan crouched beside the toilet, holding his stomach.

"What's wrong, darling?" she asked, rushing over to him.

"I'm real sick, Aunt Marlie." The boy groaned pitifully. "I threw up blood."

Marlie's alarmed eyes darted to the toilet. The bowl was a bright red.

"What?" Bryce gasped.

He would have rushed into the crowded space, too, if Marlie hadn't held him back with a hand upon his chest. She sniffed the air and detected the scent of recently sprayed room freshener and...something else. Glancing around, she spotted what she was looking for in the wastebasket—the neck of a cream-soda bottle poking out of the trash.

Marlie turned to a worried Bryce and let him see the smile she was hiding from Ryan. "Bryce," she said, trying to keep the laughter out of her voice. "I'm afraid whatever you had planned for Ryan will have to wait. We'd better call the paramedics."

Bryce's worry turned to confusion, then understanding, as his eyes followed the path of Marlie's to the wastebasket and its suspicious contents. He slumped against the doorjamb, his blue eyes dimming as they rested on the huddled child turned against him. "Yeah," he said lifelessly. "I hope it isn't too late to save him."

Marlie saw Bryce's hunger, the pleading for a glimmer of acceptance from his son. And she hurt for him. Bryce had some annoying habits, but he was a good man who loved his son. Though Bryce's triumph would mean her defeat, she was driven by justice to see his pain end.

"Oh, Ryan's a tough little rascal, Bryce," she said, telegraphing him a look that invited him to play this game. "He'll probably pull through."

Bryce smiled wearily, but nodded his willingness to participate. "I hope so. I was looking forward to flying with him."

"Oh? You were going to take Ryan flying today?"

"Yeah. I thought if he was interested, I'd start teaching him some flight basics."

"Well, maybe you could take me instead. I'd like to learn to fly."

An eyebrow hiked in feigned surprise. "I've been teaching you to fly every night for a month."

Marlie shot him a scowl for his risqué remark. "You weren't interested in going solo, were you?" she asked meaningfully.

Bryce laughed. "No, no. It's more fun with two, and I'll take you flying with me anytime. We can drop Ryan off at the hospital on our way to the airport. By the time we get done with your flying lesson, Ryan should be all wired up, full of tubes and ready for visitors."

Marlie nodded agreement. "I'll go get his pajamas."

"He won't need them. The nurses will make him wear one of those sissy gowns that lets his butt stick out. It's easier for giving shots."

While all this distressful planning was going on, a miraculous recovery was taking place. Ryan had perked up considerably at the mention of learning to fly and had improved steadily with the graphic description of hospital procedures. "I'm feeling better now, Mr. Powell. I think I could go flying with you," he assured him eagerly.

Bryce didn't look too convinced. "I don't know, Ryan. I don't want you to throw up blood all over my plane."

"My stomach's okay. Honest." He grinned devilishly, the look of his father definitely in his eyes. "I think eating Aunt Marlie's cooking for so long must have upset it."

"I resent that," Marlie said, laughing as she helped Ryan up. "Beat it, buster, and don't ever come back." Ryan went, laughing on his way downstairs. She swallowed hard, then turned an overbright smile on Bryce. "You play dirty, Powell, but it's effective."

In Marlie's green eyes, Bryce saw the shattered look that she couldn't hide. Her sadness was probably the antithesis of his elation. But a strange guilt rose up inside him, eclipsing his joy, leaving him discontent. Gaining from another's losses had never appealed to him. He wished he had something to offer her that could take the place of what she was giving up for his sake.

He didn't, yet he refused to believe that those beautiful green eyes would never shine with true happiness again.

Oh Art, Bryce thought, your wise words once offered me hope. Now if I could just pass them on with the same assurance that you gave me.

"Marlie," he said slowly. "A smart old man once told me that without some rain in a person's life it soon becomes a desert. I know that's small comfort coming from the man who's taking your sunshine, but it's also comes from a man who's faced enough storms that he can expound on the joys of the sun when it comes out again."

Marlie cringed inwardly, knowing how Bryce intended her to apply his philosophy to her life. "Perhaps someday I'll remarry and have children of my own to replace Ryan." She shrugged noncommittally. "Look, Bryce, I appreciate your trying to hold an umbrella over my head, but it isn't necessary. When I came to Sunnydale with Ryan, I came expecting the rain."

Marlie's confidence that she could handle her problems didn't make Bryce feel one bit better. Especially the way she mentioned handling them.

# Nine

A kid's thought process, even one like Ryan's, wasn't too complicated to figure out. Bryce remembered being a kid. When the school bully magnanimously offered free rides on his new bike, every boy who'd sworn to hate that bully forever would still line up for a ride on his bike. What Bryce was doing to Ryan was similar to what that bully had done to all the other boys: dangling an irresistible lure.

As Marlie had suggested, it was sort of a dirty trick to play on a kid. Bryce knew that Ryan wished that he didn't want to be here with him. But the lure of flying a plane was just too irresistible to pass up.

If the situation hadn't been so serious, Bryce might have laughed at Ryan's attempt to remain loyal to Marlie while indulging in a boy's dream. He was having the time of his life, and managing to do it with a contrary scowl on his face.

"If you're not having a good time learning pre-flight check procedures, Ryan," he said gently, "I can take you home."

"I want to learn the check procedure, sir," he said sullenly.

"But you don't want to be too happy doing it, right?"

"I'm not supposed to be happy when Aunt Marlie is so sad," he stated, blinking away tears. "She cries all the time, and we want to go back to L.A."

Bryce drew in a ragged breath. His son was being torn apart, sensing that his beloved aunt was in some kind of bondage. It would take an unsettling mixture of truth and lies for Bryce to hone away the rough edges of Ryan's dilemma. God forgive him, but Bryce was willing to tell those lies to bring peace to his son.

"I think you're wrong about why your Aunt Marlie cries, Ryan. I think she cries because of you."

"Me?"

He nodded. "Your poor attitude isn't making Marlie happy. Maybe if you didn't act so miserable, she'd feel better."

Ryan thought that over a moment, then turned a frown on Bryce. "But neither one of us were unhappy until you butted in," he accused.

Bryce couldn't argue that point, so he didn't try. "You're right, and I'll accept my part of the blame. Right now your aunt is mad at me because I bullied her into marrying me." He shook his head forlornly. "Don't ever bully a woman into marriage if you don't plan to watch your back, Ryan."

"Why did you do it, then?"

"Because I wanted you to be my son. I wanted it so badly that I goofed."

Plainly, Ryan didn't know how to address that confession, so he ignored it. "Suppose Aunt Marlie never likes you? Will you let us go?"

Wanting to howl with frustration and knowing he couldn't, Bryce settled for silently cursing his fate. Ryan couldn't conceive being separated from Marlie, couldn't conceive that Bryce would take him and leave his aunt. The child was negotiating for Marlie's happiness, knowing therein lay his own. To turn the child's priorities around would call for one more deception.

"I'm not a quitter, Ryan. One way or another, this family will work. A wise old man once told me that if I *act* happy, I've taken the first step to *being* happy. I gave his advice my best shot and found that he was right. I'd be willing to help you do the same thing.''

Ryan was listening now, and thinking. Bryce decided to pad the proposition. ''I'd be a good father to you and treat you just like my son. I'd teach you to throw a ball and swing a bat. I'd teach you how to fly planes and how to build them.''

Ryan's big blue eyes were shining now with excitement. ''Build them?''

''Yep. I have one of the best model-plane collections in the country. I've been building them since I was about your age.''

Ryan chewed on his lip a few moments, then blurted out, ''Would you ever spank me?''

A crucial question, apparently, which called for honesty. Bryce smiled, and replied, ''Yes. If you deserve it.''

A few more suspenseful moments passed. Finally Ryan nodded his acceptance. ''I'll give it my best shot, sir.''

Bryce expelled his breath in gusty laughter. ''Good enough, son. Let's land this baby and go home. I'm curious to see what your aunt's burning for dinner tonight.''

The chess game was put on hold that evening due to the splendid weather outdoors. Ryan chased fireflies while Marlie and Bryce stretched out on loungers to watch him. Marlie opened her mouth to speak, but Bryce beat her to it.

''The contractor called me today and said my house was ready to move into,'' he said leisurely. ''I thought you might like to do some decorating. Maybe pick out some carpets and curtains. I have some furniture at my apartment you could have redone.'' He shrugged. ''Or buy new if you want.''

Marlie's fingers dug into the metal arms of her chair. Bryce's mellow mood was just what she needed to broach the subject of her own project. ''Actually, I was hoping to take a few days to make a trip back to L.A. I'd like to get a team of my executives working on the feasibility of opening that branch of Stynhearst here.''

"You brought it up again," Bryce said in annoyance. "I thought we'd agreed to drop the subject of you traveling back to L.A."

"We didn't agree, Bryce," she said, trying to sound reasonable. "You ordered me not to go, which wasn't your right. But I'd give even a lunatic a second chance to reconsider."

"Apparently you'd give a lunatic a second chance to do just about anything," he muttered under his breath.

"Pardon me?"

Thinking about Marlie falling into Rex Kane's clutches started nausea rolling in Bryce's stomach. All that stood between Kane and Bryce's urge to hunt him down was knowing that Nick was on the case. Unless Marlie insisted on discussing the details of catching her ex-fiancé, Bryce would rather not dwell on the subject.

"You can't leave, Marlie," he said flatly. "I need you here for Ryan. So decide now whether you want to fix up the house he'll be living in, or I'll find someone else to do it."

It was dawning on Marlie that Bryce never intended to allow Stynhearst Industries to become a reality in Sunnydale if he could prevent it. What else would he sabotage with his single-minded desire to reclaim his son? Her own relationship with Ryan? Her visitation rights?

Bryce was using her until she became dispensable. Why couldn't she give up her gullible idealism and face that fact? Only indispensable people found a permanent place in this world.

So, that's what she would have to be—indispensable.

Suddenly Marlie hoped Sunnydale suffered a long-term shortage of domestic help. She'd learn to cook—and pray that she didn't kill them all first. She'd turn that farmhouse into a palace. It would be Ryan's home that she was preparing, and if she failed at indispensability, at least she would be leaving behind another reminder of her love for him.

"All right, I'll decorate the house," she said softly. "I assume I can invest my time in the project, but not my money?"

"I'm not a pauper, Marlie," Bryce snapped. "Leave your credit cards and checkbook in your purse."

"*You* have my purse," she snapped back.

Bryce sighed in exasperation. "Nick still has it. I'll try to remember to pick it up tomorrow." He lied.

In the smoldering silence that followed, the crickets chirped merrily on, a dog barked somewhere down the street and other children's laughter joined Ryan's as a game of hide-and-seek was started.

Bryce was rather disgusted with himself for allowing the discussion of what he'd hope to be a pleasant job for Marlie turn into another brawl. "Want me to help you with your batting stance?" he finally asked, holding out an olive branch.

Marlie accepted it. "It's a little too dark for that, isn't it?" she returned lightly.

"We could work mainly by feel."

"You have a licentious streak in you, Powell."

"I know. But you secretly love it."

Yes, she was afraid she did. But it was all part of being indispensable, wasn't it?


Marlie threw herself into becoming indispensable as if she were a soldier engaging the enemy. Decorating a house might have been fun had she known one thing about doing it. Since she didn't, she felt compelled to break a few of the rules that Bryce established for the project. The first to go was Bryce's rule number one: enlist only the services of local enterprises.

Well, Sunnydale didn't have an interior decorator, so she phoned New York and had one bused in. Ms. Crawford stayed one afternoon and helped Marlie pore over the fabric and carpet samples and suggest room arrangements and window treatments.

Marlie wanted only the best for Ryan's home. Therefore, she was compelled to break Bryce's rule number two: stay within the budget. Since Ms. Crawford's services cost a pretty penny, Bryce's rule number three also bit the dust: use only his money. The truth was, by the time Marlie would finish purchasing Ms. Crawford's selections, a sizable chunk of the cash she still had stashed beneath her bed would be gone. But the end justified the means: the local merchants would enjoy a windfall in profits and Ryan would have his palace.

With a new purpose and a plan firmly in mind, Marlie let the buoyancy of her optimistic spirit carry her through the next few days. Sunnydale merchants provided fast, efficient service, and the house progressed beautifully. When Bryce was unavailable, Mrs. Cobb, Nick Vaughn and even Happy Hanson were around to lend a hand with the details. Marlie was thankful for both their help and their constant company, for another furtive call to Stynhearst informed Marlie that Rex Kane had not surfaced there.

But a skulking Rex Kane soon became the least of Marlie's worries; Bryce in a rage definitely took precedence.

"Marlie!" he roared from the dining room, where Marlie had left him catching up on his personal mail. She rushed into the room, expecting almost anything but what she got.

"What are these?" he demanded, waving a fistful of papers under her nose.

"You'll have to hold them still if you want an answer, Bryce," she said.

Bryce provided his own answer. A stack of purchase statements went sailing to the floor, and Marlie's heart along with them, as he snapped out each store name at the top of the page, plus each paid-in-full total at the bottom. "Did you think I couldn't add, dear?" he growled after littering the floor with her miscalculations. "And more importantly, where did you get the money?"

Marlie cleared her throat, uncomfortably. "I figured you could add. I didn't figure the merchants of Sunnydale would waste a tree sending me a statement of a paid account."

"Marlie, Nick hasn't mentioned the bank being robbed of a small fortune, so where did you get the money to bust the heck out of your decorating budget?"

"Oh, I had a little stashed in a sock."

"You're lying," Bryce said flatly. "Maybe you have an extra checkbook or credit card in that sock, but it would take a suitcase to hold the cash you spent."

When Marlie would have interrupted him, he cut her off with a brusque "hush," and continued. "I gave you a budget for the house because it was important that you spend only my money on it. If I can't trust you to do things my way, Marlie, then I'll have to insist that you hand over that sock.''

He would have explained that Nick advised there be no traceable money transactions for Kane to track to Sunnydale, but Marlie cut in.

"I wanted to make the house nice for Ryan," she said hotly.

Irrationally, what had been stewing in Bryce's head suddenly boiled over the top. For Ryan. Everything was for Ryan. She had nothing to give him that he didn't have to cajole from her. "I'm not a millionaire, Marlie," he bellowed. "When you're gone, Ryan will have to learn to get by with what *I* can provide. He may as well start learning that *I* can't, or won't, pay for his love."

The moment the hateful words had left his mouth, Bryce regretted them. It was about the most unjustified accusation he had leveled on Marlie yet, and he was thoroughly ashamed of himself for saying it. Ryan showed little interest in material possessions; Marlie had bought his devotion with love and attention. That's what made Marlie such a tough act to follow; she had a three-year lead on her acquisitions.

He held out a hand in repentance. "Marlie—" he said, but a moment too late. She had already shut him out as she hastily vacated the room.

He gathered up the mess he'd made on the floor, while wondering about the mess he'd made with Marlie. The paid bills in his hand mocked him, as if telling him that whatever the cost of this setback, he would be the one paying for it.

A few minutes later, Marlie entered the dining room, carrying a dirty gym bag. Stopping beside Bryce's chair, she set it on the table, unzipped it, then turned to him. "You're not going to stop until you've taken everything, are you?"

Not waiting for his answer, she hefted the bag and upended it over his head. When the last bundle of crisp hundred-dollar bills had landed, she tossed the empty bag away. "There. You have it all now, and I hope you're satisfied."

The shock of Bryce's bombardment took a moment to recover from. When it did, he shoved away from the table, letting bundles of money drop to floor unheeded. "Marlie..." he began to say. But she would have none of his explanations. She backed up to the door, shaking her head in firm denial. "Hush, Bryce," she sobbed. "Just hush." Then she fled up the stairs.

The following day, Bryce, Marlie and Ryan moved to the house on the hill. For Marlie, the day arrived with none of the usual excitement expended on such monumental events. The joy of the project had died for her when Bryce had as good as accused her of buying Ryan's affections.

Bryce had banked the damn money for Marlie three days ago in an account under her married name. She needed only to sign the authorization card and pick up a checkbook, but as far as he knew she hadn't made the effort.

If she was making a silent statement as to how badly he'd screwed up with that uncalled for remark, her message was coming through loud and clear. She avoided him as much as possible, and when she couldn't, she responded to him with a smile that said absolutely nothing.

Tonight he wanted that to change.

"Marlie," he whispered, pulling her stiff body close to his, "are you asleep?"

"Yes."

He smiled and reached over to snap on the bedside lamp. "Good. It'll probably be easier for me to apologize."

"I don't want your apologies, Bryce."

"I know. You want an excuse to put those damn pillows back in bed with us, but I'm not going to give you one. What I want is to see the old Sunny shining again like she was a few days ago."

She wasn't exactly responding, but she was listening, so Bryce pressed on. "What I said about you making Ryan materialistic wasn't true. The truth is, you've done a wonderful job raising my son, and I'm grateful. I guess I sort of resented your success because it wasn't mine, and I took my disappointment out on you."

He pushed her tangled hair aside so he could see her face. "I'm sorry for what I said. Will you forgive me?"

A million years went by while Marlie lay quietly in his arms. Finally she nodded and smiled. It was another one of those Mona Lisa smiles that could be taken either way. Bryce chose to take it as encouraging.

In the following days, Marlie made a valiant effort to resurrect the old Sunny. She had to, or else throw in the towel and admit that she was dispensable. In some ways, finding happiness was an easy task. Bryce kept surprising her with his courtesy and sensitivity. She found herself admiring the things he did, his strength and determination.

For other reasons, happiness eluded her. The circumstances of their marriage still needled her, and then there was always worries of Ryan. To a little boy who'd had very little paternal attention, Bryce was a fascinating man.

Exquisite model airplanes now hung suspended from the ceiling and covered shelves and tables of an extra room in the house. When Ryan had entered that room the first time, his eyes had rounded with wonder and excitement as he gazed at the tempting delight. Bryce had scored again with the boy, and Marlie felt another small part of Ryan that had always been exclusively hers being pulled away.

To counteract the feelings of pending doom, Marlie exhausted herself with giving. She ran a marathon of activity from daylight until dark, settling Bryce's home, creating an atmosphere that lacked only the proverbial pipe and slippers. She cooked some of the most awful concoctions to ever come out of a kitchen, but she did it with such a unique flair that she dazzled her diners right out of indigestion. And for the benefit of her audience, she smiled lots of empty smiles. But on the inside, where the pain and fear refused to abate, she cried out for a reason why men only wanted to use her.

Ryan didn't know he was helping to break his aunt's heart. He just knew he loved the move from the apartment in town to the house on the hill. With everyone's attention diverted, he boldly extended the limits of his independence. He explored the open meadows and the new world of wildlife existing around the lake and in the woods by his home. In his adventures he discovered the half-mile path that led from the edge of his yard, down the hill to a vacant lot in town.

Today, the tinkling bells of the ice-cream truck echoed faintly through the trees, again beckoning the little boy away from the tedious strictures of obedience. Aunt Marlie was busy cleaning closets; he wouldn't bother her with asking permission, and he'd be careful.

Down the hill he went, answering the siren's call. As he reached the truck, he passed the same maroon car with the same driver, whom Ryan had noticed on his several other clandestine rendezvous with the ice cream man. This time, though, Ryan passed close enough to see the driver's face better through the tinted glass. There was something strangely familiar about him, as if Ryan had met the man before, only now he looked a little different.

Ryan shrugged the matter aside as he gave his order to the vendor. But on the way back up the hill, the question kept nagging him. Where had he seen that man before? Ryan ran several possibilities through his mind until one stuck.

The little boy's eyes widened. He tossed his half-eaten cone into the weeds, wiped his mouth on the back of his hand, then bolted for the house. Inside, he ran to his room and rummaged in a drawer until he found his old wallet that contained his favorite snapshots. The one he was looking for wasn't his most favorite, but today he was glad that he had kept it.

With an ink pen, he carefully drew a beard and dark glasses on the tall man standing between himself and his aunt in the photo. With a grim expression, he studied the results. "Rex Kane," he muttered fiercely.

So, Rex Kane had been spying on Sunnydale, hoping to catch his Aunt Marlie alone and convince her to return with him to California. Well, Rex wouldn't catch Aunt Marlie because she had so many friends in Sunnydale that she was never alone.

Ryan hadn't completely made up his mind about Mr. Powell, but he had about Rex Kane. Between the two men, there was no competition. Until that creepy Kane left town,

Ryan would keep his aunt away from him, just to make certain she didn't get led astray.

Ryan's new duties went into effect the following day. His aunt was riding with him and Mr. Powell to the airport, and drat, if she didn't notice a shopping center within walking distance of the terminal. Rather than wait until he and Mr. Powell were done flying, Aunt Marlie was going to the delicatessen and buy something special for dinner tonight.

Knowing he couldn't disappointment Mr. Powell, Ryan settled for giving his aunt a safety lecture; it concluded with a stern admonition of the most important rule: don't talk to strange men.

"I promise to faithfully follow all the rules, Ryan," she said, then kissed the little boy goodbye. Her smile slowly vanished as she watched him skip happily off to the plane.

Bryce leaned forward and kissed her brow. "Ditto everything Ryan just said. And don't look so worried. I'll bring him back to you."

But for how much longer? she wondered wistfully. Bryce had worked hard to win Ryan, and in the ways of little boys, he'd succumbed to the lure of flying planes and playing ball. He was following Bryce, watching him and now finally imitating the first male role model whom he had grudgingly admired. Notch by notch, the grudge had slipped away completely. The child who'd had so far to go was settling. Her Ryan had returned to his nest.

"I don't think it's working, Mr. Powell."

"What? The fuel gauge?"

"No, sir. Me acting happy around Aunt Marlie. She still looks awfully sad all the time."

Bryce heaved a sigh. So his son had noticed, too. Bryce wasn't surprised. Marlie wasn't as good at dissembling as she thought. She hadn't fooled him and she hadn't fooled Ryan.

The Sunny that Bryce had met in the alley those few weeks ago was gone. The woman he saw now was consumed with fear and depression, and he knew from experience how the futility of both could take a serious toll on sanity.

Bryce knew he was making Marlie happy in the bedroom, not that it didn't take some creative encouragement on his part. Her nerves were strung as tight as a bow and she resisted the natural urges of her body. It took no imagination to figure out the reasons why: he was making progress with Ryan and she thought she saw the handwriting on the wall.

But did she really think he was going to kick her out in the street now that Ryan was finally cooperating? Gosh, she must admire his sterling character. The truth was, after this Rex Kane mess was over, he intended to help her set up a Stynhearst base in Sunnydale if that was still what she wanted. But she'd have to be patient a little longer—and, for Ryan's sake, be happy.

"Sir?"

Bryce looked over at his son who had stopped fiddling with the control panel and was looking inquiringly at him. He was probably waiting for an answer to the problem of his sad aunt. Lord, how he wished he had one. But since he didn't, he would have to prevaricate one more time. "Ryan, there comes a time in every man's life when he has to admit his limitations. You nor I can make your Aunt Marlie happy. She has to want that for herself."

"You mean Aunt Marlie is being unhappy on purpose?"

Bryce smiled, taking Ryan's slight outrage as a good sign. The child was thinking twice now about abandoning his new life here just to running away with Marlie. "Well, maybe 'on purpose' is putting it a bit too strongly. I believe she's just not trying enough."

Ryan checked a couple more gauges, then suddenly blurted out, "I think a baby would make Aunt Marlie happy. Why don't you give her one?"

Bryce's hands instantly sprouted six sets of thumbs. He dropped his clipboard between his legs and took a long moment in retrieving it. It gave him time to gather his wits so he could address his son's suggestion. "Making babies takes cooperation, Ryan. I'm not certain I could get your aunt to do that."

"You'll never know if you don't give it your best shot, Mr. Powell," Ryan stated philosophically.

Bryce gulped. Did he really want to give that his best shot? He realized the efforts Marlie was putting out for Ryan's sake, but her efforts were rubbing off on him, too. Her domestic charade was so complete that he almost wanted to believe the fantasy she was spinning, for life had started resembling something real and tolerable.

But start another life with Marlie? Two years ago, he'd promised himself never again to allow anyone to become so entangled in his emotions that he would lose his grip on reality. He had learned the hard way that nothing is forever and losing loved ones hurts too much.

He closed his eyes and saw again Marlie turning around and walking away from him at the airport terminal today. One of these days she was going to turn around and start walking and never come back. What would it be like for him, and for his son, when she was gone?

That question hurt. And that hurt worried him.

Bryce and Ryan spied upon Marlie from around the kitchen corner as she removed a cantaloupe from the fridge and began cutting it into wedges. Halfway through the job Bryce crept up behind her, snatched the knife from her hand and tossed it onto the counter, then pulled her into a low dip over his arm and laid a wet, smacking kiss upon her surprised lips. Of course she didn't respond; Bryce hadn't expected her to.

"See, Ryan," he said, putting Marlie back on her feet. "Absolutely no cooperation."

"Aunt Marlie, you *aren't* trying," Ryan accused her, as if surprised to find this true.

"What am I not trying to do?" she asked bewildered.

"To be happy," the child answered. "You can't expect Mr. Powell to do everything."

Marlie turned to Bryce, who was studying the print of the wallpaper intently. Sensing that it was time for another performance, and that a kiss would be a requisite, she picked up the knife and whacked off the tip of the melon she'd been slicing. She looped an arm around Bryce's neck and bathed *his* surprised lips with succulent fruit before kissing it away.

Bryce sucked in a slow, steady breath while Marlie carried out her revenge. It was undoubtedly the most seductive thing she'd done to him, and darned if she hadn't chosen to perform for an audience. He pulled her more firmly into his arms and growled to Ryan, "Beat it, kid. Your aunt and I have some serious necking to do."

"What's necking?" Ryan asked.

"I'll tell you all about it in a year or two."

Ryan went away smiling.

Marlie put a little space between herself and Bryce. "If you think you've gotten rid of him after piquing his curiosity, you're crazy."

"We'll go somewhere away from little prying eyes, then," he said, backing her against the counter.

Marlie shook her head. "No such place exists. I've seen Ryan dissolve into a puddle and ooze under a crack in the door to get an answer to his question."

"Tonight, then?" Bryce persisted, wanting a firm commitment.

Marlie smiled a smile that offered no guarantees.

So, that night Bryce took no chances. He'd noticed that Marlie became a different woman in the bedroom. He also noticed that she resisted the transformation and, probably without knowing that he could tell, resented it happening.

Of course Ryan's suggestion about making a baby with Marlie wasn't practical, but the process without the product was. Therefore, he spent a good deal of each day thinking up creative ways of taking the resentment out of her surrender. He understood her position, but he understood his better and would prefer to win her over to his point of view.

With this in mind, Bryce closed the bedroom door, gathered Marlie into his arms and rocked her gently within his embrace. "Guess what we're going to do tonight," he asked, and grinned when her green eyes showed a spark of interest. "We're going to play department store mannequin. And you get to be the dummy."

"Well, thanks a lot," she said, rapping him sharply on the chest.

"The object of the game is to remain stiff, and only respond when I make you. You've been practicing that lately, so you should be pretty good at it." He stepped away from her, leaving her cautiously standing there. "Mannequins don't frown, dear. They're very dignified." With the tips of his fingers, he coaxed her lips into the look he wanted. Then he made a slow, deliberate circle around his subject, assessing very angle. "This outfit is nice, but inappropriate for evening wear," he finally said. "It has to go."

Her plaid seersucker blouse was undone with the greatest of care, as if each button was a priceless jewel. Bryce slid the garment down her arms and dropped a kiss on each exposed shoulder. The unneeded item was then carelessly balled up and tossed to the floor. A grin broke out across Marlie's face.

"Remember your dignity, dummy," he cautioned her, and the grin disappeared.

The white poplin shorts were disposed of easily. He untied the drawstring at her waist—with his teeth—and slid his fingers beneath the elastic band. Inch by excruciatingly delicious inch the shorts traveled down her thighs, her knees and her shins until both the shorts and his trailing lips ended up at her ankles.

From his kneeling position, Bryce looked up the long length of shapely legs and smiled. "Stiff," he reminded her. "You lose two points for wobbly legs."

He pointed out the offending limbs by stroking the backs of each kneecap with his fingertips. Marlie thought she just might collapse on top of him if he didn't cut it out. "Darn," she gasped, and tried to stiffen her noodley knees.

Bryce saw to it that she failed. "We don't want you to feel left out, now do we?" he asked the leg he'd neglected on his trip down her body. So his mouth made the return journey up the other leg. Once again topside, he rubbed his hand over her soft, smooth midriff and whispered, "They just don't make dummies the way used to. Thank goodness."

While he nibbled on a handy earlobe, his finger hooked under the front closure of her bra, and with an adept flick of the wrist, left the lacy mauve confection dangling on her elbows. The bounty the bra had hid filled his hands, and he nibbled that, too, until he had to hold Marlie on her feet.

The matching mauve panties went the way of the shorts, but on the return trip home, Bryce discovered something he hadn't found on previous travels. His tongue traced the slight ridge of scar that arched with the curve of her hipbone. Intrigued, he inspected the small flaw, then, with questioning eyes, looked up at Marlie. Here was a mannequin in its most realistic form. She stood stiff, her only response, a quivering lower lip.

"What happened?" he asked, frowning.

Marlie closed her eyes, her breath coming deep and choppy. "I met an ugly man with an uglier knife," she murmured.

"Kane?" he breathed, and when she nodded his fingers unconsciously clinched into the flesh of her hips. He didn't know what to say to Marlie, but he knew what he wanted to do to the man who'd hurt her. Soon, he vowed silently, but now was not the time. He was losing Marlie to a recall of abuse that he couldn't even imagine, but could spare her these moments of renewed anguish.

He lifted her in his arms and kissed her trembling lips. "I won't share you or my bed with any other man, not even in memories, Marlie," he whispered hoarsely. "Forget him, and remember where I can take you."

He lay her on the satin sheets and would have abandoned the silly game of the past few minutes, but Marlie possessed a stronger will than Bryce would give her credit for. She needed to forget Rex. She wanted to remember stardust. She smiled. "I didn't remain stiff, so I guess I lost the mannequin game." A bit startled by her own boldness, her gaze caressed the fly of his jeans where she noticed his interest in her hadn't waned. "But I think we still have a winner," she whispered.

Bryce laughed triumphantly and stripped off his clothes, flinging them helter-skelter across the bedroom floor, then joined her between the layers of satin. He had her beneath him before she could catch her breath, but there was no rushing the preliminaries. Once he'd claimed his territory, he slowed the pace so as not to miss one tiny speck of her flesh.

His hand stroked her nub of sensation; his fingers leisurely checked for signs of progress. His mouth stayed busy from her chin downward, and somehow he even managed to find stimulating chores for his foot and knee. The man appeared as if he had settled in for a long night of delicious torment, but when Marlie grasped his shoulders, gritting her teeth against the results of his careful ministrations, she felt tremors racing through his heavy muscles and sweat sheening across the broad slope of his back, belying his casual control.

The devil made her do it. She wanted to see that casual control blow sky-high, even if it cost her some pleasure of her own.

As it turned out, it didn't. Stroking, petting and nibbling Bryce Powell wasn't a sacrifice, it was a confirmation of man and woman's compatibility, a celebration of connubial communion as it was meant to be. She wrapped herself around him, urged the linking of their bodies and resounded his appreciative groans of rapture. The pace predictably picked up tempo until both were submerged in mindless bliss, finding heaven, then haven, one more time in each other's arms.

Later, Marlie snuggled into Bryce's embrace and gave up all pretense of self-deception. She wasn't becoming an indispensable person to this man, but despite Rex's lessons, she had gained another indispensable person in her own heart's entourage.

In her oh-so-clever plan to make her place in Bryce's home, she'd managed to fall victim to her own device. She was trapped by yearnings her mind had not authorized but her heart embraced. As grandly ludicrous as the possibility should have been, Marlie Stynhearst Powell had fallen in love with her blackmailer.

# Ten

___

"Mr. Powell?"

"Yes," Bryce answered, reaching across the cockpit to check Ryan's seat belt.

"You're my real father, aren't you?"

Every muscle in Bryce's body froze. Thoughts splintered in a thousand directions, leaving indecision to flourish in a frightening void. With one little word he could put the years of separation behind them. With one word, the pain, the longing, the hopeless dreams would disappear, and he would be a father again. He opened his mouth to speak, but that one word trembled in fear, refusing to articulate itself.

As if sensing Bryce's difficulty, the child reached out and patted his hand. "You are, aren't you?" he repeated gently.

It was the wealth of compassion and understanding in the child's voice that pulled Bryce's faith together. "Yes," he said quietly.

Ryan nodded. "I thought so. The evidence was rather overwhelming."

"What convinced you?" Bryce asked, finding his son's clinical analysis a calming influence. Elation started to bubble in his bloodstream with flamboyant effervescence.

"That silver horn, for one thing," Ryan answered. "Aunt Marlie told me it belonged to your son. But every time I looked at it, it was like I'd seen it before, but that was impossible. But it wouldn't have been impossible if it had belonged to me."

"That's brilliant deducting, Ryan," Bryce said, grinning and itching to get his hands on the child.

"Yeah, but that wasn't all."

Bryce smiled. "No? What else?"

"You, sir. The way you acted. I've been around stepparents before. They treated their stepkids okay, even real good." He shook his head. "But something about the way you treated me was different. It was like nothing would be right unless I was *really* happy. I think that's how a real father would be."

Ryan shrugged with such maturity that Bryce felt his heart would burst. "I wanted to be sure before I did something dumb, like ask you if I was your son, so I snuck up to the attic and went through that box where I'd found the little horn. There was a book full of baby pictures. Some of them looked just like some of the pictures of me that Aunt Marlie carries around in her wallet." His voice conveyed hope as he concluded with, "It all added up to you being my real father."

"And how do you feel about that?" Bryce asked gently.

"I'm glad, sir."

"Glad enough to allow your dad a hug for all he's missed?"

Grinning from ear to ear, Ryan unbuckled himself and made a lunge across the space between them. The happy clinch was long and satisfying and ended with two sets of blue, tear-glistening eyes staring rather dazed at one another.

"I'm real glad, sir," Ryan repeated before his eyes drifted away from his father's face. "But..."

Bryce urged his son's chin back around. "But...?"

"What about Aunt Marlie?" the child whispered.

Bryce closed his eyes and sighed. Yes, what about Aunt Marlie? He couldn't see himself being less than honest with his son at this point. "I don't know, Ryan. She said she'd stay until she was certain you were happy."

"And if she goes, I won't be going with her?" It was a question plus its answer, spoken with heartbreaking uncertainty. Bryce hated to add to that fear, but he had to. "No."

Ryan's brow furrowed in deep concentration for several moments. Then he said, "I guess I'll just have to pretend that I'm not happy, then."

Bryce slumped back against his seat and blew out a gusty breath of frustration. Being reunited with his son hadn't ended all his problems. He had suspected for a several days now that it wouldn't. Holding Ryan in his arms had lifted an old burden, had replaced a chunk of himself that had been missing too long. Yet something else was still missing. Bryce suspected its recovery could be found wherever Marlie was.

Ryan's idea for keeping Marlie around would work for a while, but not forever. Bryce had realized this when he'd thought up a similar version of his son's plan. Making Marlie happy had slowly crept into the same category as making Ryan happy. But accomplishing this act wasn't his son's responsibility. Bryce knew the fix was within himself. *He* had to make Marlie want to stay.

"I think I've bullied your aunt enough, Ryan," he said slowly. "I'd rather try to convince her to stay without using any more dishonesty."

"But suppose you can't," Ryan said desperately. "Suppose she leaves with Rex Kane and we never see her again?"

Bryce's heart stalled with either of Ryan's grim possibilities. "She won't be going anywhere with Rex Kane, Ryan," he said firmly. "But—" and here, his faith began to waiver "—if Marlie can't be happy with us in Sunnydale, then we'll have to let her go."

Ryan clutched at his father's broad shoulders and quietly wept his fear and grief. Bryce held on to him firmly, and for some foolish reason, felt tears of distress dampen his own cheeks.

"Don't worry, Dad," Ryan said, his wobbly voice fighting for control. "I'll think of something."

Bryce felt sort of silly for nurturing a hope that his six-year-old son would do exactly that.

The first time Marlie heard Ryan address Bryce as Dad, she thought her life would end with the next heartbeat. In a way it did. Marlie's part was over; the admission of Bryce and Ryan's true relationship would be the final act in the drama, and it would be merely a formality. The bond between father and son was strong and could survive the confession.

Day after day, Marlie waited to receive her walking papers, hiding with remarkable success the twisting pain she felt as she contemplated her future. The future she wanted was with a darling little boy and a blackmailing husband, and she wouldn't be surprised to find she'd do just about anything to retain possession of both.

The magnitude of this revelation was profoundly tested. When Marlie wished to stay far away from Bryce until her betraying senses redeemed themselves, a series of strange calamities threw her constantly in his path.

Her ear-piercing scream brought Bryce on the run for the first incident. When he came to a screeching halt in the kitchen, it was to stare at Marlie, his mouth agape.

Finally he asked, bewildered, "What are you doing up there?"

From the top of the refrigerator, Marlie pointed a shaky finger at the flour bin where a tiny mouse happily frolicked in the contents.

Bryce looked into the bin, ignored the mouse and instead asked with interest, "Did you scream before, during or after you climbed onto the refrigerator?"

"I didn't climb, I leapt," Marlie informed him, derisively. "Any woman can leap five feet straight up when she's provoked."

A skeptical eyebrow lifted at her boast, but he didn't say a word as he found a paper cup into which he scooped the flour-dusted intruder. "I don't like rodents, Bryce," she warned him.

He nodded, set the cup on the counter and reached up to grasp her waist. "You've seen your last," he promised as he lifted her from her perch and let her slide down the length of his body.

"Thank you," she said breathlessly. She wasn't certain whether her respiratory state had been due to her fright, her provocative descent from the refrigerator or Bryce's resulting kiss.

It didn't really matter.

It didn't matter the next day when the lids on every glass jar in the pantry refused to budge regardless of how she pounded and soaked them. Bryce came, Bryce fixed, Bryce kissed her. It didn't matter when the refrigerator mysteriously unplugged itself. Bryce came, Bryce fixed, Bryce kissed her.

Bryce's excellent restorative powers kept Marlie's respiratory condition in a state of perpetual acceleration. To have such a man underfoot heightened her awareness of him. Her heart tangled in a web of love and its extraction would surely destroy her.

Bryce was aware of many things, too. He knew that his son had been a busy little beaver the past few days, executing schemes that would throw his father and his aunt together. Bryce had to grin at some of his son's ploys; they weren't bad for an amateur. Gluing lids onto jars, unplugging an appliance from an outlet only a small arm could reach and introducing Buford the mouse to the joys of the flour bin were all designed to demonstrate to his Aunt Marlie how much she needed his father.

If Ryan's schemes hadn't accomplished that, it certainly had accomplished the reverse; his father needed Aunt Marlie. Since marrying her, the old yearnings to raise a family had begun to invade his solitude. A man could commit a great deal of himself to others without giving everything away. As long as he kept a sensible perspective, there was room in his life now for someone else, and Marlie was the perfect choice. That night, Bryce paced the floor at the foot of their bed and complacently lectured Marlie on the dubious logic of his vision of marital bliss.

"Ryan knows that I'm his real father, Marlie," he began bluntly, concluding that the shock treatment would quickly gain her attention.

It didn't. Not with so much as a blink of her eye did she react adversely to the news, but merely rearranged the sheet over her lap and nodded.

Rather nonplussed by her attitude, Bryce cautiously pressed on. "I know you consented to marry me because—" When his word choice did induce a reaction—her eyebrows raised in outrage—he brusquely corrected himself. "Okay, you *reluctantly* consented to marry me because you wanted to see Ryan settled and happy. But now that that time is here, *I'm* reluctant to have it end."

Marlie continued to stare at him, sedate expression and relaxed posture putting an exclamation point to her tepid acceptance of his declaration. Bryce's insides tightened to the point of pain. Marlie wasn't interested in extending their marriage. What did he do now?

Marlie was such a beautiful woman, inside and out. All his senses approved of her, having no more sense than a happy puppy chasing a milkweed fluff. A man with a suspicious nature could find reason to believe this bit of fluff was deliberately taunting him with what he was drooling over. Perhaps she was. It wasn't as if he'd given her much reason to like him.

But all that could change if she gave him the chance. Ryan would be his bargaining chip. "My son may call you his aunt, but he thinks of you as a mother. I'm his father, so that makes us a family." He turned away from Marlie, so he wouldn't have to face her outrage over his next mandate. "All things considered, I think it best that we stay married."

Marlie smiled sadly at the strong back turned against her. Her victory felt so hallow. *Oh, Bryce, where is the love to justify your conviction?*

At that moment, Marlie knew she had enough love to supply the world. With no theatrics and no lecture, she shared her own conviction in two softly spoken words. "All right."

Bryce whipped around, his arms dropping to his side, his face registering shock. "All right?" he repeated, needing confirmation of what he thought he'd heard.

Marlie smiled, nodded and opened her arms to him, welcoming the blackmailing scoundrel who thankfully had robbed her of dreary choices. And he came to her, surrendering his body to the pleasure of hers.

"Hello, baby," a male voice whispered into Marlie's ear. She smiled, but didn't open her eyes as she shifted on the lounger where she lay drowsily basking in the afternoon sun. The smile waivered when cold metal pressed against the fabric of the T-shirt covering her breasts. Her eyes flew open and she saw that the bearded face of the man squatting beside her did not belong to her husband. "Rex," she breathed.

"In the flesh," he replied, stroking her temple with the barrel of a nasty little gun. "Did you miss me?"

"Like ulcers," she said, amazed at her calmness. This final meeting had been inevitable, and she was glad to see it come. Her only worry was getting Rex away from the house before Bryce or Ryan could walk into Rex's firing range. She glanced at the weapon in his hand and commented leisurely, "I see you're taking your life of crime more seriously these days."

Rex chuckled softly. "I've missed your sense of humor, darling. I'll reacquaint myself with it on our little trip."

"Where are we going?" she asked, getting to her feet as she followed the instructions issued by the motion of his gun.

"First we're going to get away from here. I've had to keep a low profile, waiting for a chance to catch you alone. But until now, you were constantly surrounded by people." He chuckled. "That's what I get for involving myself with such a popular little socialite. Anyway, we're going to retrieve the copy of the original tape that you stashed somewhere here in this disgusting little burg. Then we're going to L.A. to retrieve the original you stashed in a safety-deposit box at the bank."

*Think, Marlie, think,* she ordered herself. What could she tell him to get him away from here? She wanted him running for his life, as she had run these past few weeks. She wanted him constantly looking over his shoulder, worrying about his future. "There's only one copy of the tape, Rex, and I gave it to the police."

Rex grinned. "If I believed that, Marlena, you'd be dead right now."

Marlie licked her dry lips and tried to put some starch into her wilting backbone. Rex really was taking his life of crime more seriously—from kidnapping to blackmail to murder. It would be just a matter of time before she ended up dead, if Rex found out that she had passed along that tape. She didn't know what Pryce had done with the copy he had taken from her, but she assumed it was somewhere in the house. And the house was the last place she wanted Rex.

She nodded resignedly. "Okay, Rex, you've got me. I rented a locker at the airport in Hartford and left the tape in it," she said, which was the truth. She had made two copies of the tape and scattered them around, not realizing how smart a move that was at the time.

"If you're telling the truth, Marlena, you might just live to see that kid again. No one can prove I had anything to do with the boy's kidnapping, so once I've destroyed the tapes, it will be your word against mine that the taped confession ever existed."

He urged her across the yard and to a path that led down the hill toward town. "Let's get to the airport before I'm spotted. Shooting you here would be damned inconvenient."

"I'd just hate to inconvenience you, Rex," she said sneering, dodging exposed tree roots in the path.

"You've already done that, darling," Rex answered, giving her a little jab in the back with the gun. "If I wasn't so angry with you now, I'd admire your extraordinary enterprise. Laying a false trail to Canada for me to follow was clever. Except for one small detail," he added, patting her consolingly on the shoulder. "When I got to Winnipeg and found the cupboard bare, I knew you had tossed me a red herring to buy time. I asked myself, why would my prim and honorable little Marlena need to buy time, and where would she go?"

He answered his own question with smug confidence. "Why to Sunnydale, of course. Her wearisome little conscience would demand that she take the kid back to his father. But, wait!'' Rex dramatically intoned. ''What was to become of the devoted little mother hen if she gave her chick to the rooster?'' He shook his head. ''Too sad of an ending to the tale, hmm, Marlie? The mother hen first needed to make a place for herself in the nest, then joyfully reunite the chick and the rooster.''

Rex grasped Marlie's arm, his fingers bruising her flesh. ''Then the mother hen could turn over the wily fox to the authorities, couldn't she?'' he jeered. ''You've done a splendid job so far of living out that fantasy, darling, but I don't much care for the ending. So I'm going to change it. If you cooperate in getting the tapes, I may let you bring Ryan back to L.A. to live with us. If you don't cooperate, I'll kill him.''

Marlie suddenly felt cold, despite the scorching August heat. Rex really was insane. She would be a fool to believe he'd let her go after he'd recovered the tapes. One witness to his crime would be one witness too many. Her only advantage was that he didn't know how firmly she'd established herself in the Powell nest. His ignorance would buy her time, but somewhere between Sunnydale and Los Angeles, Marlie had to escape this lunatic.

She and Rex left the woods and entered a vacant lot near the center of town. Marlie looked around. Where were all the people who had constantly been with her these past weeks? Why wasn't Nick patrolling the streets, or Happy Hanson rumbling around in his truck or Mrs. Cobb walking her dog? Now that she desperately needed their companionship, she felt very much alone.

But she wasn't alone.

Ryan was exercising his independence again, and luckily spotted his Aunt Marlie coming down the hill in time to duck behind the front of the ice-cream truck.

Ryan crinkled his brow in consternation. She was with Rex Kane! Ryan wondered what had gone wrong. Yesterday, his dad and Aunt Marlie had told him that they had worked things out, that they were going to be a real family. Ryan thought there was actually going to be a happy ending, like in those dumb fairy tales.

He watched his aunt get into the Saab with Creepy Kane and drive away with all his dreams. Well, he wasn't going to stand for it. Barf Dater Eliminator may be out of uniform, but he was still on duty. He hightailed it back up the hill and found his father in the basement, putting up some shelves that Aunt Marlie had wanted.

"Dad," he said determinedly. "If another man came along and tried to steal Aunt Marlie from you, you wouldn't like it, would you?"

Bryce stopped in midmotion of lining up a bracket and looked at his son. "No," he said slowly. "I don't think I'd like it much at all."

"You'd go after her, wouldn't you?"

A spurt of fear jetted into Bryce's bloodstream. "Ryan, is some man trying to steal Aunt Marlie from me?" he asked pointedly.

"He's already done it, if you don't do something."

"Who?"

"Rex Kane," the child spat out contemptuously.

The bracket slipped from Bryce's nerveless fingers and clattered to the floor. He grasped the child's shoulders. "You've seen Rex Kane with Marlie?"

"Yeah. About ten minutes ago she got into a car with him and drove away."

"Where did you see them, Ryan?" he asked, unable to keep the edge of panic from his voice.

Ryan told him what he'd seen, and had barely gotten the last words out before his father was thundering up the stairs. By the time Ryan had joined him in the kitchen Bryce was hanging up the phone, grabbing Ryan's hand and towing him to the car.

The mile and a half to Sunnydale provided the most thrilling ride of Ryan's life. Nick Vaughn met them in front of the police station, where they transferred to a patrol car.

"Do you remember the color of the car your aunt got into with Rex Kane, and which way they left town, Ryan?" Nick asked calmly.

"Sure. It was a dark red car, just like Dad's, and they went that way," he replied, pointing west.

Nick put the information on the radio as he screeched away from the curb. "Don't worry, Bryce. We'll catch them."

Bryce slammed his fist into the dashboard. "We shouldn't be needing to catch them," he raged. "The plan was perfect. Having Marlie and Ryan watched constantly was supposed to prevent this. And what happens? On my damn day to watch her, the bastard slips in. But how, Nick? How? Everyone in Sunnydale had seen that photo of Kane and knew he was dangerous. How did he get past everybody?"

Ryan leaned over the front seat. "Dad? Rex Kane is dangerous?" he asked hesitantly.

Bryce ran agitated fingers through his hair, regretting his forgetfulness of little boys with sharp ears. "We'll get Marlie back, Ryan," he said reassuringly. "But, yes, Kane isn't a very nice man."

Ryan thought a moment, then said, "Rex has a bushy beard now. And driving a 9000 Turbo Saab like yours probably tricked everybody into thinking it was you behind the tinted windows."

Bryce and Nick exchanged glances. Chuckling, Nick got back on the radio with the new information and got an almost immediate response. A Saab of that description had been spotted at the airport in Hartford.

"We've got him, Bryce," Nick said confidently.

But they hadn't.

The wily fox eluded the airport authorities. Nick, Bryce and Ryan got to the airport in time to watch the small jet containing Kane and Marlie wing its way over the city. Bryce stood beside his son and watched the small craft crest the western horizon, feeling as if a significant part of himself was tied to the rudder.

A small hand grasped his, and a sniffle drew his attention. Stooping down, he gathered Ryan into his arms and tried to think of some trite words of comfort that would help them both.

"I forgot to tell Aunt Marlie that I loved her this morning," Ryan sobbed. "Aunt Marlie says its important to always say the words, because you never know when you'll be sorry that you lost the opportunity." He raised his tear-streaked face to his father. "She was right, Dad. I wish she was here now, so I could tell her that I love her."

Bryce had to gasp for breath, feeling the impact of Ryan's words like a body-slammed to the concrete floor. Lost opportunities. How well he knew them. He was beginning to think he was too much an idiot to know what to do if he found one. He'd left Marlie believing that all she could expect was his half-baked notions of commitment. What else could she believe? She'd accused him of not being satisfied until he'd taken everything from her and she was right; he'd wanted it all. But fool that he was, he'd neglected to take the most important thing of all—her love.

Now, if Marlie didn't come back to him, he would have forfeited his opportunity because he'd been too much a coward to gamble again. The thing was, he knew now that loving Marlie wasn't a gamble. She was strong and capable and independent, yet willing to share the best of herself with those she loved.

She'd offered that love in so many ways that a blind man couldn't have missed it. Bryce wasn't blind, just too slow. He prayed he'd have the opportunity to correct that serious flaw.

He patted his son's back and whispered, "Don't worry, Ryan. God willing, soon we'll both get to tell her that she's loved." He looked up at his friend standing near them. "Tell Ryan that's right, Nick," he demanded quietly in despair.

But mutual concern read the same way in both men's eyes: Marlie's survival was precarious if Kane wasn't apprehended before he got the tape. To insure his freedom, he'd destroy the evidence, plus the only witness.

Nick said, "Every place that Kane would go in L.A. has been staked out, Bryce. He still doesn't know that we're on to him. He'll walk into one of our traps."

And Marlie would be in the middle of it—that message read the same way, too.

Bryce, Ryan and Nick would have felt a lot better about Marlie's safety if they could have watched her rescue force in action. She walked beside Rex through the automatic doors at the L.A. airport and felt someone grab her from behind. Before she could even yell, she was pulled to the floor and covered by the heavy weight of another body. She heard a brief scuffle, a lot of cursing, and then she was being helped to her feet. Rex, with hands cuffed behind his back, was being led away.

A while later, she turned over the tape and newspaper article to the authorities and was a bit surprised that the man she dealt with had very few questions to ask her. She had expected to be grilled to the limit for any part she may have played in the crime, but they seemed satisfied with her story and would contact her when she was needed again.

Now that she was back in L.A., Ryan and Bryce seemed a million miles away. Her time spent as a wife and mother in a cozy domestic setting seemed fraudulent now and better off behind a closed door in her life. Someday she would see Ryan—and Bryce—again. She had to believe that, or go mad.

After father and son were settled, maybe she could see through her original plans. The feast of marriage had not really been hers to devour, but she'd gladly nibble on the crumbs of friendship rather than starve.

She should never have agreed to marry Bryce, no matter what the threat. By doing so, he was giving up the right to find a woman he could truly love, a woman who could become Ryan's mother.

Her and Bryce's marriage had happened too quickly and was plagued by circumstances that were impossible to forgive and forget, circumstances that she had helped to create. It was best if she quietly bowed out of Bryce's and Ryan's lives now. In time, Bryce's wounded heart would heal and he would begin searching for a mate to share his life. That she wouldn't be or couldn't be that mate left her limp with heartache.

To fight her loneliness and pain, she buried herself in a set of Stynhearst account books that she found in Rex's safe. For three days, she and several trusted accountants reviewed the books thoroughly and found that a great deal of the original Stynhearst assets and revenues had been channeled into some shady enterprises.

It would take months of auditing to get the complete picture of the disastrous affair, but Marlie could already see that it would take a great deal of money to make restitution for Rex's crimes. In the end, her personal worth would be drastically reduced. It seemed symbolic of her entire existence.

But at her bleakest hour, when every thing Marlie possessed seemed lost, Bryce walked through her office door. The dim light from her desk lamp cast his face into shadowy planes, and she couldn't see his expression. Her senses tracked him, alert to every nuance of his presence. Bryce had come. But why?

Leisurely he turned to shut and lock her office door. He sauntered to her desk and leaned forward, resting his weight on his arms. He spoke in jovial menace. "There's a little boy back in Sunnydale who's driving his old man nuts by blowing a silver horn and chanting, 'Born of faith, love and joy/ My child, don't be forlorn/Play for us your song of hope/ Upon this silver horn.' Ryan thinks that will get you back. I'm here to see that it does. So, I hope you have everything in your purse that you'll want from L.A., Marlie."

Excitement pumped through her veins with such enthusiasm, she thought they might explode, but her voice gave nothing away. "*You* still have my purse, Bryce."

Straightening abruptly, he shoved his hands into the back pockets of his jeans. "Well, good. It won't take as long to drag my runaway wife back home, then, will it?"

"Am I going back home?"

"Yes, you are." He watched her intently. "When you didn't come back after Kane was apprehended, I decided to give you two weeks to come to your senses and get your... cute little bottom back to Sunnydale where it belongs. Yesterday, I decided one week would be long enough." He sighed. "Six hours ago, I decided three days had been too long."

Rex's gun hadn't frightened Marlie as much as this moment did. Tongue-tied and confused, she got up from her desk and slowly walked around it to stand before him. She didn't get too close. She'd learned the hard way that it wasn't wise to get too close.

Bryce was through with distance, though. He pulled her into his arms and held on for dear life. His hands touched her, threading his fingers through her hair while smoothing it back. His lips played over her face, and his heart thundered against her breast. She returned his embrace, touch for touch, and at last knew exactly what to say. "Bryce, I love—"

Bryce put a shushing finger over her lips. "No. Let me be the first to say it. You deserve that much, Marlie."

He took a deep breath and let it out slowly. "The day I married you, I allowed you to believe that I would let you go once I had what I wanted. That was a lie, Marlie. When I married Janette, I believed that marriage was until death do us part. I never stopped believing that, but my faith got snowed under some unbearable pain.

"Good old Art helped me do a lot of digging out, but he didn't bother telling me that I could find love again if I looked for it. He probably knew that was something that I would believe only when I found it. I bet, though, if Art had known what an arrogant, stupid ass I could be, he'd have rubbed my face in it." He rested his cheek upon the top of Marlie's head and rocked her gently. "I wish he had." He whispered, "Do you think if I say the words, *I love you,* that you might want to stay with a huge disappointment like me?"

Marlie smiled into Bryce's shirtfront. He'd just pumped her full of helium, and if let go of her now she'd float right to the ceiling. She snuggled in closer and murmured, "I suppose if I'm to ever get my purse back, I'll have to go with you."

"Is that the only reason you'd come back?" he asked wistfully.

She loved teasing him. "Well, you do still owe me a cook."

"You can keep your own cook, Marlie," he said seriously. "I can move AirShip to the West Coast. L.A. is home to you and Ryan, and my home is where the two of you are."

Marlie cleared her throat and pulled away just a bit to fiddle nervously with his shirt buttons. "That's very generous of you, Bryce. I hope you can stay that way after I tell you my news.''

"What news, dear?'' he asked, catching her hands and lifting them to his lips.

"I'm practically broke,'' she said starkly. Bryce went on about the business of kissing each of her knuckles as if she hadn't just dropped an atomic bomb between them. She took heart and explained. "Rex ruined Stynhearst. I'll be lucky to salvage enough revenue to keep the L.A. office open. If I'm extremely lucky, I can still build a smaller branch in Sunnydale.''

Bryce wasn't being very attentive to explanations, but seemed intent on removing her dress. "Well?'' she demanded, pulling her hair aside so he could get at the zipper.

"Wonderful. Sunnydale or L.A. Either sound wonderful if you're there.''

"Sunnydale, definitely,'' she said, stepping out of the pool of material at her feet. "I'd miss Mrs. Cobb's cooking lessons, Happy's truck stalled in the middle of the street and Nick's flirting with me, just to see if he can rile you.''

"He can,'' Bryce said absently, bending down to slip her shoes off her feet. "Okay, we'll live in Sunnydale.''

Marlie put a hand on his broad back to keep her balance as she cooperated with the operation. "But what about my money?''

"You said you only had a few lousy million left to invest in Stynhearst.'' The lingerie and hosiery came off in one fell swoop. He stood back to admire his handiwork as he added, "What other money are you talking about?''

Marlie suddenly couldn't remember, and said so as she started helping Bryce with his too many buttons. When she had him in the same state of delightful indecency, she led him to the large chesterfield at one end of her office. She pulled him down over her and urged a merger more satisfying than Stynhearst and AirShip could ever hope to match.

"What can I give you, Marlie? What do you want?'' Bryce asked, setting a rhythm of love that drew her into music composed in the soul.

"I want to fly with you, Bryce Powell. I want to gather stars and touch angel wings. I want you with me always."

"I love you," he whispered against her lips.

"Yes. That's what I want," she whispered back.

Later, as the two lovers lay entwined, they looked into each other's eyes and marveled. Who would have thought their lives' richest treasures would be found in Pothole Alley.

*     *     *     *     *

# SILHOUETTE® *Desire*

**HAWK'S WAY**—where the Whitelaws of Texas run free till passion brands their hearts. A hot new series from Joan Johnston!

Look for the first of a long line of Texan adventures, beginning in April with THE RANCHER AND THE RUNAWAY BRIDE (D #779), as Tate Whitelaw battles her bossy brothers—and a sexy rancher.

Next, in May, Faron Whitelaw meets his match in THE COWBOY AND THE PRINCESS (D #785).

Finally, in June, Garth Whitelaw shows you just how hot the summer can get in THE WRANGLER AND THE RICH GIRL (D #791).

Join the Whitelaws as they saunter about HAWK'S WAY looking for their perfect mates . . . only from Silhouette Desire!

# SPRING FANCY

**Three bachelors, footloose and fancy-free... until now!**

Spring into romance with three fabulous fancies by three of Silhouette's hottest authors:

## ANNETTE BROADRICK
## LASS SMALL
## KASEY MICHAELS

When spring fancy strikes, no man is immune!

Look for this exciting new short-story collection in March at your favorite retail outlet.

Only from

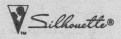

**where passion lives.**

**What a year for romance!**

**Silhouette** has five fabulous romance collections coming your way in 1993. Written by popular Silhouette authors, each story is a sensuous tale of love and life—as only Silhouette can give you!

Three bachelors are footloose and fancy-free...until now.
(March)

Heartwarming stories that celebrate the joy of motherhood.
(May)

Put some sizzle into your summer reading with three of Silhouette's hottest authors.
(June)

Take a walk on the dark side of love—with tales just perfect for those misty autumn nights.
(October)

Share in the joy of yuletide romance with four award-winning Silhouette authors.
(November)

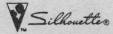

**A romance for all seasons—it's always time for romance with Silhouette!**